HEARTS IN PERIL™

A Chilling Reunion

Jan Fields

Annie's®
AnniesFiction.com

Library of Congress-in-Publication Data
A Chilling Reunion / by Jan Fields
p. cm.
ISBN: 978-1-64025-649-1
I. Title
                    2023930192

AnniesFiction.com
(800) 282-6643
Hearts in Peril™
Series Creator: Shari Lohner
Series Editor: Amy Woods

10 11 12 13 14 | Printed in China | 9 8 7 6 5 4 3 2

Prologue

*T*he heavy wooden door opened without a sound, making the woman smile. She had been concerned that someone would hear her, but the grand house was meticulously kept, right down to silencing squeaky doors or floors. She stepped out, leaving the door open behind her. Her slipper-clad feet were silent as she padded down the hall, her gown almost floating around her. If anyone saw her, they'd be certain that she was a ghost. *Wouldn't that be perfect?*

She rested a hand on the rail of the grand stairs and walked down them slowly, imagining admirers waiting at the bottom, glasses raised in a toast to her. In her mind, she was barely in her twenties again and almost too beautiful to bear. Everyone wanted to see her, or be her.

She slipped through the imaginary admirers and continued wandering from room to room in the great house. From the foyer, she heard the wind raging outside, furiously slamming against the thick walls, desperate to get inside, to get at them all. She shivered at the sound and drew her ethereal robe closer around her, though the house was warm enough.

She moved silently through paneled halls, stopping to open every door. The rooms within were shadowy but not truly dark. Most were faintly lit by small lamps. It was likely that she wasn't the only person prone to wandering at night.

She paused now and then, striking theatrical poses and smiling for her imagined audience. Eventually she reached the conservatory. Laying a trembling hand on the levers to open the door, she paused. Should she go in? With its abundance of tall windows, the space was certain to be cold, but what could be more romantic than a conservatory?

Somehow she could not resist. She stepped through the door, and immediately a chill nipped at her, slipping through her thin gown and sinking deep into her fragile bones. She could even feel the cold of the stone floor through her slippers. She wouldn't linger. The room was less romantic than depressing after all. There were no pots of flowers defying winter—simply bare floors and straggling remains of desiccated plant life in cracked and broken crockery. The room held far less than she had expected, though she spotted a stone bench in the far corner and considered resting there. It would be a lovely picture with the storm lashing the windows behind her, but it was too cold to pretend anymore. She suddenly longed for her warm bed. Surely the walk had tired her enough to sleep.

That was when she heard the door to the conservatory open again and realized one particular door in the house actually did squeak—a startling anomaly in the otherwise silent house. She spun with a smile, hoping against hope for the admirer she'd been dreaming of. But admiration was not what the figure in the doorway had in mind. Not at all.

*T*hough the New England coast was as picturesque as Poppy Hayes had hoped, she'd seen enough clapboard buildings perched on uneven rocky ground for one day. After being on the road since daylight, Poppy wanted nothing more than to be out of the car and on to the adventure that awaited. She tried to think of every new job as an adventure, an opportunity to dive into the life and memories of another person and bring the moments back to life. That was what ghostwriting was all about, at least as far as she was concerned.

At the age of thirty-eight, Poppy had finally made it through the growing pains that came with launching into a ghostwriting career, though she still remembered the days of not enough work and too many bills. Back then, her family had hinted in phone calls and emails that perhaps Poppy should find a different job, something steadier and more lucrative, but she had persevered. She loved ghostwriting, especially when she was hired to write someone's memoirs. She felt as if she were being given permission to ask nosy questions and poke into interesting lives. In some ways, her vocation gave Poppy the chance to try out different lives, as she immersed herself in stories someone else had lived.

Her current subject promised to be particularly interesting. Mariette Winter had been as mysterious as she was wealthy for all of her eighty-plus years. It wasn't that the public hadn't wanted to know more about the poor little rich girl. When Mariette had been young and astonishingly beautiful, the press had hung on her every word.

Though she'd steadfastly avoided the media, she made enough appearances to prove that she was more than a trophy wife to her industrialist husband, Joseph Winter. Mariette had a keen mind and quick wit, and she used both to deflect questions rather than answer them. But at long last, the woman was ready to tear away the veil of mystery and tell all in her memoirs, and Poppy was going to do everything in her power to help.

A bend in the road revealed another clapboard-clad village—Bainbridge, the last of the day. She'd arrived in the nick of time. Stray snowflakes were beginning to fall, and she had no desire to navigate the twisting New England roads in the precipitation. Bainbridge was the village where Poppy would catch a small ferry that would take her to Winterhouse Island, a place nearly as famous as its owner. The entire island belonged to the Winter family. The family mansion was the sole building on it as far as Poppy knew, aside from the dock for the ferry. If there *were* more buildings there, she supposed she'd find out soon enough.

Following street directions recited by the bossy computerized voice coming from her phone, Poppy wove her way through the village. Some of the directions made no sense, taking her on what appeared to be the most convoluted route possible, but Poppy had no way of navigating on her own, so she followed each command until she reached the shore and the ferry dock.

Poppy pulled off the road into a snow-dusted gravel parking lot. A sign announced *Ferry by appointment only*. Her gaze flicked to the clock on her dashboard. She was almost exactly on time for her appointment. "It's all coming together," she murmured.

She would have to leave her car in the village. The ferry didn't carry vehicles, and the car would be of no help on the island anyway. It had no roads. Winterhouse Island promised to be isolated, possibly even desolate, but whether that meant Poppy would find it unique and exciting or claustrophobic and dull, she couldn't yet say. One thing she didn't doubt was that she was in for a challenge with her unpredictable client.

The crunch of gravel under her vehicle's tires grated on her worn nerves, and Poppy noticed she was gripping the wheel far more tightly than necessary. She pulled into an empty spot, then took her hands off the wheel and shook them out. Before she shut off the engine, she noticed that her gas tank was nearly empty. She'd cut the time close for the ferry, so she had no chance to track down a gas station in the village. Hopefully someone would be able to aim her in the right direction when she was done with her work on the island.

She hopped out of the car, her sensible black boots sinking into the gravel. The chill was already seeping through her footwear, and she wished she'd worn thicker socks. She would really be cold on a boat speeding across the water. She tugged her coat closer around her and noticed the snow had stopped. *Good.* After hauling her bags out of the trunk, she locked up the car. The blare of a boat horn, low and commanding, pulled her attention to the end of the dock beyond the ferry sign. There was one boat bobbing gently in the water—an ancient, battered fishing vessel that appeared older than the photos she'd seen of Mariette Winter, and not nearly as well preserved.

"Well," Poppy muttered to herself as she trudged toward the aging boat. "You wanted some excitement. A ferry that barely floats should be positively thrilling."

To her surprise, she found a small group of people standing on the dock near the ferry. Apparently others were also traveling to Winterhouse Island. She studied each person as she approached. She recognized three of them, though all were significantly older than Poppy. Not one of them could be younger than seventy.

Her attention was especially drawn to a tall, handsome man in a long, tailored wool coat, wearing a cold expression. She's seen the same features staring out from cover photos on several of the business magazines she read regularly. Cecil Lewis was sometimes referred to as the king of the modern robber barons, though probably not to his face. He was ruthless in business and nearly as tight-lipped as Mariette.

The woman who shivered beside the businessman was Jacqueline Lamarr, the actress. As a fan of old B movies, Poppy knew Jacqueline had once been beautiful and relatively popular. She'd been in several horror films, cast for her vulnerability and her impressive scream. She still acted, though she no longer played the imperiled heroine. These days, she was much more often cast as a creepy old lady or enigmatic crone.

She didn't strike Poppy as particularly scary at present. She had obviously taken considerable care with her appearance, especially her makeup. Poppy caught a glimpse of the beautiful woman Jacqueline had once been, despite the unattractively sulky visage she wore at present. Jacqueline oscillated between the two men with her. Cecil paid Jacqueline no attention at all, but the second man watched her closely and sometimes even touched her arm and murmured to her.

Poppy knew the second man too, though not from upscale business magazines. There was nothing glamorous about Teddy Marcone, other than his wealth. He was a tall, stout man whose clothes had been made to fit but still couldn't match the robber baron's elegance. His hair was an unnatural shade of blond for a man his age, and his face was ruddy and flushed. Teddy was rumored to be the biggest hitter in organized crime to ever manage to stay out of prison. He was wily and dangerous. Poppy couldn't imagine a more unlikely group than the three who stood on the dock, and their apparent familiarity with one another was unexpected as well.

This job is growing more interesting by the minute. Poppy could hardly wait to find out what was ahead for them on the island, so she pasted on a cheerful countenance and hauled her luggage the rest of the way to join the group. A fourth person, shorter than either Cecil or Teddy, stood apart from the others, and he wasn't the least bit familiar to her, but Poppy guessed he was the ferry captain by his carefully crafted crusty-old-salt guise. He wore a rough beard and a long, dark gray raincoat over several layers. Everything about him was worn and weathered. He was a man with no interest in giving the impression of either prosperity or elegance.

Finally close enough to hear the captain's rough voice, Poppy realized he was trying to talk the others out of taking the ferry. "You'll be trapped on the island when the blizzard hits," the captain warned. "I'll not take my boat out in rough weather."

"Blizzard?" Poppy said as she reached them. "The last weather report I heard said the bulk of the storm was going to pass us by."

The captain laughed, though there was no mirth in it. "Don't believe the weather forecasts, Miss. New England storms will do what they please, and this one wants to do damage."

"Captain Andrews," Cecil said in a tone that suggested rapidly thinning patience, "if there is some issue with the weather, we shouldn't stand around chattering. We are going to the island. We have paid the fee. It is your job to provide the ride. End of conversation." By the end of his speech, Cecil's tone had grown so cold that Poppy's skin prickled at the hint of a threat lying slightly below the surface.

"Fine," the captain grumbled. "Suit yourself. But don't expect me to be your bellman. You'll deal with your own luggage." He crossed his arms over his chest mulishly.

"Idiot," Cecil said, his voice probably too low to reach the captain, but Poppy was closer. The elegant man picked up his suitcase, then frowned at Jacqueline's pile of luggage and sighed. He picked up her larger suitcase and strode past the captain toward the boat.

Jacqueline called her thanks after him, but he didn't respond except for a brief nod. She fluttered her hands over her smaller suitcase, and Teddy bowed slightly in her direction and snagged the bag, hauling it along with his own. He passed the captain too closely, bumping the other man with his shoulder. Poppy seriously doubted it was an accident.

Jacqueline gave Poppy a bright smile, making her the first of the three older people to acknowledge Poppy's arrival. "It's all in how you handle them," she said with a wink. Then she sashayed toward the boat.

Poppy chuckled under her breath, shifted her duffel higher on her shoulder, and tugged her own large suitcase. The captain took a step toward her, and Poppy thought he was going to volunteer to help her, but she quickly realized she was wrong.

"You should leave while you can," the captain said, standing so close to Poppy that she could feel his breath. Poppy didn't bother explaining that she wouldn't get very far, not with a near-empty gas tank.

Instead, she tilted her head and studied the disheveled man. "What do you mean?" she asked. "The storm? It's not a problem. I'm going to be on the island for a couple of months at least."

The captain shook his head. "Winterhouse Island is a cursed place. Everyone knows that. There's been a curse on the land since the lighthouse was first built, and the evil has only grown worse since the Winters bought the place. That old lady never comes into town. Some think she can't, that she's tied to the island by the evil deeds she and her husband committed. If she leaves the island, she'll die."

"An interesting theory," Poppy said, suppressing the urge to roll her eyes. "But 'everyone' may need a better source of entertainment than watching horror movies and gossiping."

The captain scowled at her and jabbed an oil-stained finger toward her nose. "Mark my words, girl. If you go out there, you'll be scarred in exactly the same manner as everyone else on the island."

"I suppose that's a risk I'll have to take, since my job is on that island," she said.

The captain harrumphed. "Suit yourself. But I don't expect I'll see you alive again."

Wow, what a fun guy, Poppy thought. "As I said, it's a risk I'll have to take."

He waved an impatient hand toward the boat. "Then get on board. We have to get going."

Poppy almost laughed at the man's suggestion that *she* was the one holding up the whole operation. She hiked the strap of the duffel up higher on her shoulder again and strode past him, putting as much confidence as she could into her posture and gait. She was embarking on her best work adventure yet, and she wasn't going to let a ferry captain, who was probably grumpy at having to go out in the cold, rob her of the excitement she'd felt a few short minutes earlier. Of that, she was determined.

Thomas Nordwich stood almost rigidly still, resisting the urge to shake his elderly grandmother. Though he knew it should be, it wasn't concern for injuring her that kept him from following through on the thought. At eighty-five, Mariette Winter was still far from frail, even with her illness doing its awful work in almost imperceptible ways. No, Thomas didn't shake his grandmother because she would find his frustration amusing. She knew she was being absurd, and she reveled in it. That was what frustrated Thomas the most.

"This dinner party is a spectacularly bad idea," Thomas said, recognizing that his tone was prim, but helpless to change it. "Second only to your decision to write your scandal-ridden memoir in the first place."

His grandmother groaned theatrically. "Haven't we had this conversation enough times already?"

"Are you aware of what this book will do to my mother?" Thomas asked.

"How would I be?" Mariette demanded. "She's not speaking to me. Pay attention, Thomas. I invited your mother to come for the weekend so she could have a chance to voice her displeasure. She never replied. That means Bethany has forfeited her right to complain, as far as I'm concerned." Then her voice lightened. "Unless, of course, she arrives with the others."

Thomas snorted. "Pigs might fly."

"If the wind picks up much more, they actually might," Mariette said. Her eyes twinkled in amusement, and Thomas felt some of his annoyance with her drain away. He did love his grandmother, despite her exasperating behavior.

Still, even knowing he had no chance of changing Mariette's mind, Thomas found he couldn't help picking at the problems in front of him. "You know my mother has sworn never to set foot on this island again."

"It isn't my fault that Bethany is continuing to act childish and petulant."

She's acting like you. Thomas deemed that thought unhelpful and shoved it aside in favor of trying a different tack. "You always told us, told everyone, that you would never write a memoir because the things you knew could get you killed. Is it really wise to invite the people you plan to write about here for the weekend? Things could get dangerous."

"Oh, Thomas," Mariette said with a surprisingly youthful laugh. "I was being dramatic when I talked about my memoirs potentially placing me in danger. You know how I love drama." She shook her head. "Honestly, most of the truly dangerous people in my stories are long dead. The ones who remain are too old to cause mischief."

"You're proof that there is no age limit on creating mischief," Thomas said dryly, prompting another laugh from his grandmother.

"Then it's a good thing you're here to keep me safe while I work on this book."

"A tall order," he said.

"Then it's a good thing you're taller, isn't it?" she teased.

He resisted the urge to argue. He was putting his life on hold to be here and keep his grandmother as safe as he was able, but it's not as if his life was all that exciting to begin with. He was still teaching history at the same private college where he'd worked for decades. His own wildly popular book about mysterious deaths throughout history was far in the past. It was still in print, and he made decent money from the royalties, but he hadn't yet come up with a good subject for a second book. The administration had even given up on reminding him that a new release would be terrific publicity for the college.

A less-than-vibrant career wasn't his lone source of disappointment. Thomas had always hoped to find someone special to build a life with, but that hadn't happened yet. He mostly dated colleagues, and never seriously. *Maybe my life needs shaking up*, he reflected.

"Perhaps the people you invited won't even show," Thomas said. "There is a blizzard moving in, after all."

"Really?" Mariette sounded entirely too pleased to hear the news.

"Arthur thinks so." Arthur Kent was basically Mariette's butler, though his duties were far less rigidly defined. He'd been working for the Winters since he was a young man and was beyond old enough to retire, but he'd shown no interest in leaving his employer. His sort of loyalty was uncommon, but then, Mariette paid well for it.

"Then I wouldn't doubt it," Mariette said agreeably. "That should make things interesting. I expect none of the people I invited will be put off by the weather. All they have to do is get here and they'll be fine. This house can withstand anything."

"Didn't the builders of the *Titanic* make a similar claim?"

Mariette grinned, enjoying the sparring match. "As you well know, the core of this building is a lighthouse that has stood through nearly two centuries of storms. Your grandfather had this place built with the same kind of meticulous care. It'll survive the end of the world."

"Are you ever wrong?" Thomas asked her.

"No, and you'd do well to remember it," Mariette said. "Besides, if my guests have to stay longer, all the better. I've ordered extra supplies to be ready, and it will give Poppy a chance to get to know them, which will help with the book."

"Poppy," Thomas said with a snort. "What kind of name is that for a serious writer?"

His grandmother's sparkling amusement was gone in an instant. "I'm appalled by your behavior, Thomas. Cattiness is such an unattractive trait. If you find Poppy's first name too frivolous, you may call her Miss Hayes. And I expect you to treat her with flawless respect and cordiality."

"Of course." He was surprised by his grandmother's sudden change of tone, but he had to admit that her loyalty to the people she employed was one of her more appealing traits.

"You know, it's your fault I had to hire Poppy," Mariette said. "You have more than enough skill to write my memoirs with me. You are the one who refused."

Thomas huffed. "My mother is having enough trouble handling the idea of your memoir without my being the one who writes the thing."

"In that case, you'd best be extra careful not to pick on Poppy. If you do anything to make that dear girl quit, I will be extremely disappointed in you."

He opened his mouth to tell his grandmother that he wasn't so rude but snapped it shut when a sound drew their attention to the closest window. Someone was ringing the heavy bell at the boat dock, the one Mariette had Arthur install so the house would know whenever the ferry made a delivery or brought Mariette's doctor. The house was a considerable distance from the dock, perched as it was on higher ground to protect it from the rising tides during stormy weather. Sound carried easily up to them.

Mariette crowed with delight. "That must be my guests. Go down and greet them. And be especially nice to Poppy, do you hear? No trying to scare the poor thing away."

"I promise, if she runs away in terror, it will be your guests who are to blame, not me."

Mariette flapped her hands at him. "Go on, then. You'll need to hurry. I expect they'll want help with the luggage. There will probably be more than you can carry at once, so tell everyone to leave their bags. You can make several trips."

Thomas knew better than to argue and merely saluted. "The Winterhouse bellman is on his way."

He grabbed his heavy coat from the rack next to the double front door and shrugged into it as he headed out. Stepping from the cozy warmth of the front entryway into the winter chill outside was enough to make him gasp. The temperature was dropping, suggesting an ominous change in the weather. Arthur might have been right. A blizzard could well be on its way.

As he strode along the path to the winding stone steps down to the dock, he pulled his coat tight around him, doing up the buttons and then pulling on gloves. By the time he reached the dock, he was well bundled, though already cold and eager to get back inside. He saw three extremely well-dressed older people milling around and stamping their feet. Beyond them was a slender younger woman who stood with her back to him, watching the ferry pull away from the dock.

On the dock lay a scattering of luggage, though Thomas was glad to see it wasn't nearly as much as he'd feared. He trotted down the short pier, ready to introduce himself to the group, but then froze, when the young woman turned around and their eyes met.

I know her!

The memory of exactly how he knew her didn't materialize immediately, but he was almost mesmerized by the sight of her. She was beautiful. But he didn't get much time to think about either her beauty or her familiarity, as Poppy Hayes marched up to him and slapped him right across the face.

$\mathscr{P}$oppy regretted her rash behavior the instant her palm connected with the tall, handsome man's cheek, and she stared in horror at Thomas Nordwich, almost unable to believe she'd struck someone on her first day of work on a new project. The slap had been automatic from a long-held anger against the almost arrogantly confident man. She was so fuzzy with shock that she barely registered the braying laugh of Jacqueline Lamarr behind her.

Then the whole experience became even worse as Poppy realized who the man must be. She had known that Mariette's beloved grandson was named Thomas, but she'd imagined he was Thomas Winter, not Thomas Nordwich, author and miserable egotistical dolt. She pressed her stinging palm to her chest. How long would it be before Mariette fired her for assaulting her grandson?

Poppy had only met Thomas once, several years ago at a faculty party held by some prestigious private college. The memory washed over her.

She didn't want to be there. She loathed that sort of pretentious affair where academics tried to one-up each other with all the subtlety of yipping Chihuahuas, but she'd come at the behest of a potential new client, the vice president of the college.

She hadn't yet signed a contract with the vice president, but he'd hinted that he would pay her handsomely to write his memoir, and she needed the money. So she milled around, chatting with a variety of people and trying to be pleasant and patient. One never knew, after all.

One of those people could be her client's best friend, someone who would be important to the work. She shifted her gaze toward the door every time she heard it open, but the vice president had never arrived at the party.

She was about to throw in the towel and go home to count her packages of ramen noodles for entertainment when the door opened again. Poppy felt a last, tiny surge of hope. It wasn't the vice president, but it was a face she recognized—Thomas Nordwich.

She was thrilled. She'd read and enjoyed his book, And Then They Were Gone. About five years older than her, the man already had a bestseller. It was no surprise his book sold so well. It was brilliantly written. She especially admired the way the author had brought the lives of long-dead people into focus and made the reader care deeply about and even relate to each of them.

Still, for all the brilliant writing, Poppy had disagreed profoundly with his conclusions about one of the deaths he'd explored. She'd done some digging on her own and discovered that a research team had done new analysis on the person's remains in the previous month. At the party, Poppy wondered what Thomas Nordwich thought of the results of that research.

Excited to speak to him, she wove her way through the crowd and soon reached the man's side. "I read your book," she gushed. "And I loved it, but . . ."

Poppy would live to wince at the memory of her enthusiastic babbling. She didn't even introduce herself before gushing about her own ideas and the independent research she'd done.

Thomas was immediately dismissive of her viewpoint. She realized that he probably wasn't aware of the new research, but his casual rejection of her thoughts infuriated her. So she laid out her case right there, louder and more forcefully than the situation warranted. More and more of the partygoers drifted over, drawn to the potential drama as she made her case.

Finally Thomas admitted she was probably right, though his tone was stiff. It was clear he didn't appreciate being shown up in public. He excused himself, and she felt embarrassed, which made her angrier. She left shortly after he did.

By morning her embarrassment had morphed into regret. She'd been so caught up in being right, and he had been so annoying and dismissive. Still, she knew she hadn't exactly taken the high road. The real blow came that afternoon when her potential new client, the vice president of the college and no doubt Thomas's friend, had notified her that he would not be needing her services. He was going with a different ghostwriter.

Poppy never doubted for a second that Thomas had pulled strings to put an end to her job in retaliation for showing him up at the party. Sure, she hadn't behaved the best when they met, but that was no excuse for taking away a lucrative job. She wasn't wealthy, and losing a project she'd been counting on was no small thing. She'd even lost her apartment when she hadn't been able to pay the rent. She'd had to sleep on a friend's sofa until she lined up another job.

But what would a rich, entitled creature like Thomas Nordwich care about making her homeless?

Even now she felt the simmering anger bubbling beneath the surface, restrained mostly by her realization that she'd made the wrong choice again. Was Thomas going to be the reason she lost another good job?

No, she told herself, refusing to pile the blame on him when she was the one with the stinging palm. He wouldn't be the cause. Her temper would be. Slapping him would be the cause.

The situation grew worse as she thought about it. The temperature had dropped steadily on the ferry ride over. She no longer doubted a storm was coming and they were certain to be stuck on the island for a few days at least. *Won't that be great?* Stuck here with all of them after

Mariette fired her. At least she had savings. She wouldn't be couch surfing or eating ramen for months if the Winter memoir slipped through her fingers.

She lifted her chin and met the man's eyes. No point mourning the inevitable. She would make the best of the weekend and do it with style. She would rise above it all. After all, she was in a unique and exciting situation with unusual people. The atmosphere fairly crackled around her. It was the sort of situation Poppy adored, so she'd simply enjoy it while it lasted.

"Miss Hayes," the tall man said calmly. Poppy could see his cheek reddening where she'd hit him, but the corners of his mouth curled up. "Welcome to Winterhouse."

It seems we're all going to pretend we're having a do-over. I can do that. Poppy beamed at him, her cheeks aching from her forced smile. "Thank you. I'm glad to be here."

She almost laughed aloud at his open astonishment. She knew he hadn't expected the sudden change in her demeanor. She didn't get to find out what he would have done next, because suddenly Teddy Marcone stomped forward and pushed past her to stand in front of Thomas. "Why isn't Mariette here? We've come a long way, and I don't appreciate being greeted by the help."

Thomas's pleasant tone and expression never wavered. "My grandmother is waiting up at the house. She is happy that you've arrived, as I'm sure she'll tell you."

Cecil called out from behind Poppy, "Teddy, stop bothering the man and let's get to the house. It's freezing out here."

Teddy spun and though his ire was focused behind her, Poppy felt a zap of alarm at the fury in the man's face. "Don't tell me what to do."

"Good to know you've grown old without growing up," Cecil replied, his tone as icy and flat as Poppy already expected from him.

She recognized him as a man who rarely let anyone see what he was really thinking and feeling. "Can we get going now?"

"What's your hurry?" Teddy said as he pushed by Poppy. "You are in an awfully big rush to see Mariette."

"I'm in a hurry to get out of the cold," Cecil said. "You are the one bringing up her absence."

"She isn't absent," Thomas cut in. "She's at the house waiting for us."

"You think you're so sophisticated, Lewis," Teddy said. "You're no better than me. You never were."

Cecil chuckled. "Don't be a buffoon, Teddy. That ferryman is better than you."

At that, Teddy threw a punch that would have done some harm if it had connected, but Cecil stepped smoothly out of the way and drove his fist into Teddy's stomach.

The sudden violence horrified Poppy. She'd been hoping for drama, but watching two elderly men succumb to fisticuffs was too much. However, she noticed that the violence did not have the same effect on Jacqueline, who watched the fighting with an eager, unveiled glee.

Thomas hadn't been expecting a quiet, peaceful weekend. He'd known better. But still, he couldn't have imagined being slapped by a beautiful woman he barely knew or breaking up a geriatric fistfight. Yet, when the situation called for it, he waded in and pulled the two men away from one another.

"This is not the time," he insisted.

Apparently Teddy Marcone did not agree that it was not the time, because he threw another punch, low and hard. Somehow Thomas managed to step into it, blocking the blow from landing on its intended target, Cecil. Instead the man's substantial fist drove into Thomas's rib cage. And it *hurt*. He bit down, refusing to cry out, and used his greater height and youth to drag Teddy away from Cecil.

"My grandmother is waiting," Thomas said, pleased that he managed to keep most of the pain out of his voice. He was going to feel that punch all weekend.

"Teddy, stop being so silly," Jacqueline said as she walked over to slip her arm through Teddy's. "Let's go up to the house. I'm positively freezing."

Teddy grunted. "Fine." He pulled away from the woman and stomped over to grab his suitcase, then stormed off in the direction of the house. Thomas suspected the climb up the steps would take some of the wind out of the man's sails, which would be good for them all.

His own suitcase in hand, Cecil walked past Thomas. "Sorry for that. Teddy always was a boor."

Thomas didn't respond. He was glad to get everyone moving. He scanned the area for the luggage. Poppy had already picked up hers, and he could tell by the way she held the bags that they were packed full, but Jacqueline sidled up to him. "Are you going to help with my luggage? It's far too much for me." She gave him a sly side glance that Thomas assumed was supposed to be coquettish but came closer to distressing. It wasn't that Jacqueline wasn't a handsome woman, because she was. In fact, her resemblance to Thomas's grandmother was striking. But she was old enough to *be* his grandmother. She would do better to save her eyelash fluttering and side smiles for the men who had come with her.

"I'm here to help," he said simply as he grabbed her two bags. With a wink, she hurried off, calling out to Cecil to wait for her.

Thomas felt the ache in his chest increase from the weight of the suitcases. The walk up so many stairs wasn't going to be much fun.

To his surprise, Poppy fell in step beside him, dragging her wheeled suitcase and carrying a slightly smaller bag on her shoulder.

"Are you all right?" she asked. "That was a pretty solid punch."

"I'll be fine," he said, though Poppy was right. It had been a solid punch. He felt fairly sure Teddy hadn't managed to crack his ribs—surely he wouldn't be breathing so well if the man had, but the pain was significant nonetheless. He glanced at her. "Considering you hit me first, I'm not sure you have room to be aghast at Teddy."

"I slapped you," Poppy conceded, "but I didn't punch you. I could have, but I didn't."

"I stand corrected," he said. "Again." He certainly remembered the woman who walked at his side, despite having never heard her name on the night when she'd schooled him so thoroughly at the wearisome faculty party years before.

"I am hoping this won't have to be awkward all weekend," Poppy said as she ambled along beside him.

"My getting beaten up by my grandmother's guests?" he asked, and found he enjoyed the sound of her laugh in response.

"Actually, I meant our previous encounter," Poppy said. "But I should warn you, I now know your ribs are sore, so you should keep that in mind before you decide to give me any trouble." The smile she beamed up at him was dazzling, making him feel slightly breathless.

He was bewildered by the woman. Her sudden shift from slapping him to ambling at his side and teasing him left him feeling off-balance and almost dizzy. Though, that could simply be the punch he'd taken. When he'd met Poppy at the faculty party, he'd been struck by how witty and intelligent she was. He could see that she was likely to keep him on his toes for the duration of their stay on the island.

He considered asking her why she'd slapped him. He still couldn't quite work out what had prompted it. Sure, they'd had a spirited argument years before, but he was the one who'd come out of it looking foolish, not her. She'd been correct about some missed research in his work, though he could have done without her calling him out so publicly. But he'd respected her steadfastness and unwillingness to back down. For months afterward he'd hoped to see her around the campus, but he never had.

As they climbed the stairs, Thomas wished he had a spare arm to carry Poppy's bags. The steps were fairly steep, and there were a lot of them. But she never complained, soldiering on until they reached the first landing where the stairs changed direction to hug the hillside. Poppy stopped and set her larger case upright. "I'll have to come back for this one. I can't carry both at once."

Thomas waited, not wanting to leave her behind. "I'll come and get it after we bring these up."

"That's kind of you," she said. "But I don't mind returning."

He didn't want to argue, so he merely nodded, and they climbed the rest of the way together.

When they finally reached the house, Mariette was standing in the expansive foyer before the grand staircase, not far from where he'd left her to go and fetch her guests. Teddy, Cecil, and Jacqueline had arrived ahead of Thomas and Poppy, and they were glaring at Mariette in a way Thomas found ominous. He wasn't eager to break up any more fights or collect any more bruises of his own.

"Thomas," Mariette said, her eyes twinkling. "Poppy. I'm glad you could join us. Interesting how you young, agile ones were last to arrive."

"We carried the most luggage," Thomas said smoothly. He recognized his grandmother was baiting him. She was a woman who was born to poke the hornet's nest whenever she had the chance. She proved it with her next words.

"Welcome to Winterhouse," Mariette said. "I hope your stay will be a happy one. I'm glad to see old friends as always." She focused on Jacqueline, who stood almost touching Cecil. "And I'm impressed, as always, by your dedication to imitating me, Jacqueline. I assume you bought your coat after seeing my photo in *Fashionable*. Poor dear, you couldn't have known I never wear that coat anymore. I gave it to charity." Mariette's expression became one of pity. "Unless that's where you got it. I assume the roles available to you these days don't pay that well, do they?"

Instantly furious, Jacqueline took a trembling step forward. "Liar. It's you who are always copying me. It always was."

Mariette laughed at that as if it were positively hilarious.

Thomas groaned. What was his grandmother doing?

Jacqueline took another step toward Mariette, and Thomas tensed in case the actress was going to attack his grandmother. He really didn't want to be forced to haul one woman off the other. But Jacqueline merely announced, "I don't know why someone didn't kill you years ago."

Mariette laughed again, unperturbed. "Who knows, dear? This could be your weekend."

Jacqueline narrowed her eyes and spoke in a voice colder than the wind off the water. "Maybe it will."

*P*oppy had visited a number of beautiful places over the course of her career. After all, individuals who could afford to hire a ghostwriter usually had considerable disposable income and lived in luxury. Still, Winterhouse stood out as one of the most magnificent homes she'd ever seen. When they'd walked up to the house, she'd been struck by how much the tall building resembled a fortress, with its stone walls and the original lighthouse rising like a high tower. Winterhouse had many windows, but they were all tall and thin, adding to the feeling of an old castle built to withstand attack from pillagers.

Once indoors, she wondered if the house were built less to keep people out than to trap people in. It was a silly thought, and she shook it off. She was still shaken from the venom evident in the interaction between Mariette and Jacqueline. At least she understood why Mariette had laughed when she told Poppy on the phone that the coming weekend would be a gathering of "old friends." Poppy doubted there was an ounce of warmth among any of the guests.

Mariette and Jacqueline eyed one another in stony silence for a moment, then Poppy's employer changed tack entirely, and she beamed at them all. "I hope you had a pleasant crossing on the ferry."

"That tub doesn't exactly qualify for the term 'ferry,'" Cecil growled.

Mariette responded cheerfully. "That's because it's not a ferry unless I need it to be one. The rest of the time Cass Andrews takes people out fishing, when he can find tourists who'll put up with his grumpy demeanor and wild stories," Mariette said. "And I rarely have need to employ him. When I have reason to leave the island, I take my own boat. It cuts down on the village gossip about me."

Based on her chat with the captain earlier, Poppy didn't think Mariette's plan was working.

"Then why didn't you come and collect us yourself?" Teddy asked, his voice booming in the foyer.

Mariette spoke sweetly to him. "Because my boat is too small for a group this large with all of your luggage." She opened her arms. "And you made it, so I cannot imagine what is bringing on all this bluster."

"I hope you intend to take us back to the mainland in your boat when this is over," Jacqueline said.

"We can talk more about that later," Mariette announced. "For now, I'm sure you all want to see your rooms. I think you'll find them more than adequate. This house may appear rather austere from the outside, but I assure you, we have every comfort."

Jacqueline sniffed. "I'll believe that when I see it."

Mariette ignored her. "My housekeeper, Mrs. Bing, will show Poppy and Jackie to their rooms. They're not far from mine. I thought it would be nice to have all the girls together."

"Charming," Jacqueline said, acid in her tone.

"Thomas will show Teddy and Cecil to their rooms," Mariette continued. "You'll be in rooms near him. If you need anything, feel free to let him know."

Thomas cleared his throat, one eyebrow raised sardonically. "I didn't know I was to serve as concierge this weekend."

"Surprise," his grandmother said brightly. "At any rate, if any of you find your accommodations lacking, be sure to speak up."

"No worries," Jacqueline said. "I'm not prone to suffering in silence."

"You never were," Cecil said, earning a glare from Jacqueline.

"While you are settling in, I'll make a call to Matthew Bellamy.

I invited the dear man to our gathering, and he promised to attend. I'm afraid he must have missed the ferry. If so, I'm sure you can dash over and collect him, Thomas."

"If the weather doesn't worsen before then," Thomas said agreeably.

"As if you'd let some rough weather slow you down."

Thomas shook his head, his focus never leaving his grandmother. "I've been here enough times in winter to respect the weather. If the storm moves in, Matthew will have to wait it out in the village."

"We'll see," Mariette said. She flapped a hand at him. "Now, get everyone settled."

No one moved. "That is concerning about Matthew," Cecil said. "He isn't prone to being late, especially not following a summons from you, Mariette. You've always been Matthew's greatest weakness."

"I don't know what you're implying, but I think it's probably offensive. Matthew is a friend, but he also recognizes that agreeing with me is usually the smart choice."

Cecil snorted, and Poppy spoke up to prevent the conversation from getting uglier. "I need to collect my other suitcase," she said. "I had to leave it on the hillside stairs. Trying to carry both up all those steps has made me aware I ought to exercise more often."

Mariette reacted to that immediately. "You shouldn't have had to carry your own bag. Thomas, run down and collect Poppy's bag."

"I can get it," Poppy said, but Mariette ignored her as if she hadn't spoken.

"I thought I was showing your guests to their rooms," Thomas said.

"Arthur can do that." Mariette's gaze swept past the group, peering into a room beyond. "Arthur, please show Teddy and Cecil to their rooms."

"Of course," replied a large man with broad, if slightly stooped, shoulders. Poppy suspected Arthur would prove even taller than Thomas if he straightened up completely. He must have been imposing in his youth, which was long gone. He had to be at least seventy. Still, he moved with purpose and composure as he passed through the group and headed for the stairs. "This way, gentlemen."

Cecil and Teddy exchanged glances, and something passed between them that Poppy couldn't identify, but then they followed the taller man up the stairs.

"I really don't mind getting my own bag," Poppy repeated.

"Don't be silly," Mariette replied. She waved a hand toward Thomas again. "Go on, Thomas. And don't dawdle. I may need you, depending on what Matthew says."

"Of course." Thomas's tone was dryly amused, making it plain that he was used to his bossy grandmother and not inclined to let her upset him. Poppy thought she probably needed to adopt a similar acceptance to get through the next weeks. Then she remembered the slap and the fact that she probably wouldn't have weeks at said job.

Glumly, Poppy followed Mrs. Bing toward the stairs. The housekeeper was considerably younger than the butler, younger even than Poppy, who guessed the housekeeper was in her late twenties or perhaps early thirties. Mrs. Bing had a pleasant round face and an efficient way about her. It was clear that she was full of energy and wasting none of it.

Poppy noticed that Jacqueline ignored her own luggage, edging away from the group and leaving someone else to carry them up. Poppy assumed Thomas would be given that job as well, so she snagged the larger bag, hauling it along with her own shoulder bag. Mrs. Bing gave her an approving nod and stepped onto the first of the winding stairs, completely ignoring Jacqueline's second bag.

"Let's go then," Mrs. Bing said in a bright tone. "We'll get you both settled." She started up the long curving stairs.

Jacqueline called after the housekeeper, who showed no sign of hearing her. With a huge put-upon sigh, Jacqueline grabbed her small overnight bag and headed up the steps. Poppy fell in behind her, clumping the luggage along after her. She hoped the heavy suitcase wouldn't damage the stairs and was careful to keep it away from the beautiful carved railings, but if Jacqueline's bag ended up with some scuffs and dents, that would suit Poppy fine.

As she followed the housekeeper, Poppy wondered how long it would be before Thomas spilled the beans about her outrageous behavior and got her fired. She had to admit she rather deserved it, but she wished it wasn't such a sure thing. She wanted more time to study the people around her and to enjoy the amazing house.

I won't change anything by worrying about it. She pushed down her concerns and made an effort to appreciate her surroundings as she climbed the staircase. The steps under her feet were carpeted and surprisingly plush, so they probably wouldn't do much to harm Jacqueline's suitcase after all.

When Poppy finally hauled Jacqueline's case up onto the second-floor landing, she was surprised to discover that Jacqueline had waited for her and quickly fell into step beside her. She didn't offer to take the suitcase, though. "I've known Cecil and Teddy for years," Jacqueline said. "And Matthew too, for that matter. But who are you?" She grinned. "Judging by that impressive slap, I assume you're Thomas's ex?"

"I work for Mariette," Poppy said, ignoring the remark about Thomas.

Jacqueline raised her painted eyebrows. "And you call her by her first name? None of my employees would dare."

"I'm abiding by her wishes," Poppy said. They were heading down a rather long corridor, and Poppy hoped they would reach their rooms soon so she'd have an excuse to end the conversation.

"So, what's your job?" Jacqueline asked. "Keeping the grandson in line?" The older woman actually giggled at her own joke, a sound Poppy recognized from the last horror movie she'd seen Jacqueline in. It sounded every bit as creepy in person.

"I'm sure Mariette will explain everything later." Poppy wasn't going to satisfy the woman's curiosity. She might be on the verge of getting fired, but she'd make a good employee for as long as she held the job. And it was up to Mariette to reveal her reasons for her actions, not Poppy.

"Well, you're no fun," Jacqueline grumbled. "You're probably one of those young women who thinks anyone over a certain age is frail and silly. Don't be confused. The people gathered in this house are dangerous, and that includes your employer."

"Ladies?" The housekeeper had apparently noticed how far they were lagging behind. "These are your rooms." She tapped her foot as she waited for them to reach her, then waved a hand toward an open door. "These are your rooms, Miss Lamarr. Miss Hayes, you are across the hall." Again, she waved a hand. "You will find a private bath attached to each room, and an itinerary for the weekend on the writing desk."

Poppy let go of Jacqueline's suitcase, no longer seeing any need to haul it along. Jacqueline could drag her luggage into her own rooms. Poppy was glad she wouldn't be sharing a bathroom with the actress. With any luck, she'd be forced to converse directly with the woman as infrequently as possible.

"Thank you so much, Mrs. Bing," Poppy said as she slipped past and darted into her room, then stopped in her tracks after crossing the threshold. The suite was huge and beautifully decorated in pale slate blue and ivory. The heavily carved staircase could have come straight out of a Gothic novel, but this room was bright and airy with a distinctly French slant to the decor.

Poppy crossed to the window and pushed aside the drapes. To her delight, she could see waves crashing against rocks from the window's vantage point. She could also see the dock, though not the stairs, so she had no idea whether Thomas had already collected her bag. Thoughts of Thomas made her melancholy. She'd probably wrecked her weekend and her job, and she wished she had controlled herself better. Thomas was as handsome and fit as he had been at the faculty party but not nearly as smug. In fact, he'd been far nicer to her than she'd deserved.

"Sometimes you're a bull in a china shop, Poppy Hayes," she said quietly to herself. If only there was a way to glue the broken china together.

As he closed the heavy door of the foyer behind him, Thomas leaned against the sturdy wood in deep relief. The warmth of the foyer wrapped around him comfortingly. He scuffed his feet on the mat a few more times, waiting for the chill to pass before shrugging out of his coat and hanging it on a large, twisting coatrack.

He'd be content if he didn't have to make any more trips outside. The temperature had continued to drop, and the wind was picking up. The cold had lessened the pain in his bruised ribs, but that was the one good thing he could say about it. On past visits, Thomas always enjoyed wandering around the rugged, rocky island, but the day was anything but ordinary.

He hefted Poppy's bag and started up the curving stairs. He knew which rooms were assigned to the young woman. In fact, he knew where all the rooms were. His grandmother had felt that was information he needed for some reason he couldn't fathom. Mariette

Winter was a puzzle box of motivations, and Thomas had long ago decided not to try to solve that particular enigma. He'd simply take care of her as best he could, or as best she would allow.

When he reached the long corridor, he could hear humming coming from behind the door to Jacqueline's room. She sounded as if she was in a good mood despite his grandmother's rather needling comments. Of course, Jacqueline was an actress, so he supposed her career must make it difficult to survive without a thick skin.

He tapped on the opposite door, and Poppy opened it. She'd taken off her shoes as well as her coat, and he rather admired the shade of the cozy blue-gray sweater that matched the walls of the cheery room. She tilted her face up at him, her lively brown eyes sparkling. "I'm glad to see you didn't freeze to death out there."

"It was a close call," he said.

She winced. "Sorry. I should have gotten the bag. Your ribs must be sore."

"I'm fine, and I have more experience with the hill stairs. They're getting slippery because the mist from the water is freezing on them. It's better that I carried it." He set the bag down on the floor. "Are you happy with the room?"

"It's amazing. I'm sorry I won't be here very long." Sadness shadowed her lovely face, and Thomas found he wanted to fix whatever was bothering her immediately.

"Why would that be?"

"I assume you're going to tell your grandmother about the whole slapping incident," Poppy said, and Thomas noticed her cheeks growing pink as she spoke. "Which I'm sorry about, by the way. But I'll understand if you tell her, and she decides to fire me."

Chuckling, Thomas said, "If my grandmother heard that you'd slapped me, she'd probably give you a raise for being spunky.

She wouldn't fire you. But I have to admit I have no idea why you struck me. As I remember, it was *you* who embarrassed *me* at the faculty party."

She blinked at him, her expression surprised. She opened her mouth, then closed it, then opened it again. "My behavior at the party was terrible," she said, "but getting me fired back then was an extreme course of action, don't you think? I lost my apartment because of it."

It was Thomas's turn to be surprised. His brow furrowed. "I have no idea what you're talking about."

"I was at the party to meet with the vice president of the college. He wanted me to write his memoirs, but the morning after that party, he called me and said I would not be working with him after all. I assume he was responding to what I did at the party."

Thomas burst out laughing, which made Poppy rock up on her toes and glare at him. For a second he was afraid she would smack him again, and he held up a hand as he regained his self-control. "I'm sorry. Really," he said. "I didn't have anything to do with that. The college VP was and is no great fan of mine."

"Maybe he thought I embarrassed the college?" she mused, sounding perplexed.

Thomas shook his head. "Actually, I happen to know the answer to this particular mystery, though I didn't know about the connection between Nathan Daniel's ghostwriter and the woman who made me look stupid at the party. Nathan fired you because his wife demanded it. She saw your photograph online and put her foot down. She said it was enough that her husband worked at a college full of college-age women. She had no intention of him spending months pouring out his life story to a beautiful young woman. She made him hire a man for the job."

"Really?"

Thomas held up his fingers in a Boy Scout salute. "Really. I promise. I happen to know all that because he complained about it for months afterward to anyone who stood still long enough to listen."

"Oh," Poppy said.

"I really wouldn't have done anything to get you fired," he said. "Not then and not now. You were right about my mistake in the book. And you made a good case for it there at the party. I could have wished for a more private place to have my research critiqued, but that is not and would never be a reason for me to interfere with your livelihood."

"Oh," she said again, and he wondered if that was going to be all the discourse he received from her while she processed the information. It must have bothered her for a long time to inspire a slap in the face when she saw him.

"I had the publisher change the book before the second printing," he said. "I would have credited you with discovering the problem, but I didn't know your name. I asked the vice president after I saw your photo on his desk, but he pretended he'd forgotten it."

"I didn't know any of that," she said.

"I understand," he said. "I'm sorry you lost the job. That was rotten."

"And not your fault," she said, her tone completely sincere. She obviously accepted that he was telling the truth.

Thomas was surprised by how much that pleased him. And more than a little admiring of the blush that continued to creep over Poppy's face.

"I'm sorry for slapping you," she said.

He grinned. "Don't worry about it. On such a cold day as this, it was quite warming."

Her blush deepened further, and Thomas thought the weekend was looking up after all. His grandmother's guests were generally appalling, but he was glad for Poppy's company. He carried that gladness away with him, leaving Poppy to recover from what she'd learned. Since he wasn't needed to haul any more luggage or guide anyone else to their room, Thomas headed off to his own for some quiet reading before dinner.

When he finally ventured downstairs, he found he was the first one in the dining room other than his grandmother. When he spotted the elderly woman's red, swollen eyes, he hurried across the room toward her. "What happened? Are you ill?"

"I'm fine, Thomas," she said, her voice tired. "I've simply had some bad news. You'll hear all about it as soon as everyone else arrives."

"Is there anything I can do?"

She managed a weak lift at the corners of her mouth. "No, though I am glad you're here. Did Poppy get settled all right?"

"I think so."

"Good," Mariette said. "I'll need her."

Not for the first time, Thomas wished his grandmother would be more forthcoming, but he knew how stubborn she was, so he didn't push. Instead, he watched her greet her guests as they trickled in for the evening meal. If any of them noticed Mariette's emotional state, it didn't show in their faces—not until Poppy arrived anyway. Her cheerful expression immediately morphed into concern as she took in Mariette's swollen eyes. Thomas thought well of her for her worry over a woman she barely knew.

"Before we sit down to eat, I have some bad news," Mariette said, and much of the energy present in her earlier speech was gone. She sounded old—something he didn't often associate with his grandmother. "I called Matthew's penthouse in New York. A police officer answered. Matthew won't be coming."

"Was he arrested?" Teddy asked.

Mariette shook her head. "No. He was murdered."

4

The shock of Mariette's announcement hung in the air. Though his grandmother had no real details, it didn't stop her guests from asking. Even as Thomas listened, he couldn't detect any real feeling from Cecil, Teddy, or Jacqueline, despite their having known Matthew for decades. Even Thomas felt more for the man. Thomas had met Matthew a few times when he'd come to visit his grandparents and found him a quiet man with a slow, easy smile and unlimited patience for the endless string of questions children like Thomas tended to ask.

"So the police didn't mention any suspects?" Cecil asked, drawing Thomas's attention to him.

"The detective on the phone was not forthcoming," Mariette said. "Though in his defense, I believe Matthew had been found only a short while before." Her lips trembled, but she quickly regained control. "At any rate, there is nothing we can do about it now. We should have dinner while it's hot."

"At least we all have an alibi," Teddy said, then laughed.

"That's a beastly thing to say," Jacqueline snapped, and Mariette's crackling anger made it clear she agreed.

"Don't be so pious," Teddy said, rolling his eyes. "You know we'd be suspects. Who knew Matthew better, and worse?" Again he grimaced with an unpleasant expression that hardly passed for a smile.

"You're disgusting," Jacqueline hissed. "And you always were."

"Let's not do this now," Mariette said. "Please, everyone, take your seats so Arthur and Mrs. Bing can serve the meal."

Everyone took their seats without complaint. Thomas studied Cecil, who had contributed nearly nothing to the discussion of Matthew's death. The man appeared coolly unflappable as always. He'd dressed for dinner, something less than black tie, but more upscale than the sport coat and open-collared shirt Teddy wore, or the cashmere sweater Thomas had chosen. His grandmother had also made an effort, and the long black skirt and black velvet tunic accentuated her trim figure and her starkly pale skin. Jacqueline, on the other hand, wore a knee-length polka-dot skirt, and she'd chosen a white sweater and pale blue blazer. Her hair was blonde rather than white, but Thomas suspected it might be a wig.

Arthur and Mrs. Bing sprang forward to serve the food as if they'd been waiting for the chance. The dinner was delicious, consisting of a rich lobster bisque, followed by flounder baked in parchment packets with asparagus and cherry tomatoes, though Thomas couldn't imagine where the cook had gotten the vegetables, given the time of year. The fish was served with anadama bread, a New England yeast bread made with cornmeal, sweetened with molasses, and thickly spread with butter. The food was so good, Thomas almost forgot to keep an eye on the rest of the table. Thankfully, they were as wrapped up in the feast as he was.

When dinner was over and plates were cleared, Arthur served coffee, a tradition that Thomas rarely saw outside his grandmother's house anymore. The coffee was good, but he limited himself to a sip, not wanting to spend the night wide-eyed and regretting his decisions.

Mariette stood smoothly and struck her water goblet with the edge of her spoon. "I have an announcement."

"Has someone else died?" Teddy asked, then guffawed at his own inappropriate joke.

"Not yet," Mariette retorted. "I originally called you here for this announcement. I'm writing my memoirs, and you'll all be in the book, of course, as my oldest friends."

"What's this nonsense?" Cecil demanded.

"I'm certain nothing in it will be nonsensical," Mariette replied evenly. "I'm sure you've all met Poppy Hayes. She'll be helping with the book, and I hope you'll make yourself available to her over the weekend. Her knowing such key people from my past will be helpful for her, I'm sure."

"You're making a dangerous decision, Mariette," Teddy said, his voice low. "Especially if you intend to include me in the book as anything but an honest businessman and friend of the family."

Cecil barked out a laugh at Teddy's words. "You are as much of an honest businessman as Jacqueline is an award-winning actress."

Jacqueline slammed her hand down on the table. "I *have* won awards."

"Being declared the 'matriarch of scream queens' is hardly an award," Cecil said with a sneer.

Jacqueline narrowed her eyes but didn't rise to the bait. Instead, she sat up straight and smoothed the sleeves of her jacket. "The main concern I have is that Mariette is certain to lie about me. She's always been jealous of my success."

Again, Mariette used her spoon to draw attention, banging the handle against the table. "I assure each of you that Poppy and I won't write a single word that isn't true." Then she held up a hand against response. "Don't bother with threats of lawsuits. I have made up my mind, and my lawyers are prepared for the legal onslaught, as am I. If my oldest friends won't help me with this, that's fine, but neither will you stop me."

Cecil Lewis rose from his seat, and Thomas tensed in response, unsure what the man would do but aware of an edge of danger about him. "It's clear your mind is made up," Cecil said, "and I am not such a fool that I imagine I can change it. But I have no intention of helping you with this poisonous project. I will be leaving in the morning, and I expect you to arrange my ferry trip."

Teddy hopped up without Cecil's smoothness, though equally adamant. "I agree with Cecil. This is a bad idea—a dangerous idea—and I'll play no part in it. Whatever you make up about me, you'll never be able to say I helped you do it."

Jacqueline didn't rise with the two, but her sulky gaze jumped from one man to the other. "I suppose I'll be leaving too," she said finally, though her assertion lacked the heat of either Cecil's or Teddy's. Thomas suspected she wasn't happy about Mariette's memoir plan either, but she wasn't nearly as upset. Jacqueline offered one of her dramatic sighs and added, "The weekend will be no fun if Cecil and Teddy aren't around."

"I will respect your wishes," Mariette said. "I'll call for the boat in the morning. You should be able to leave after breakfast."

"If you respected our wishes," Cecil said, "you wouldn't be writing a book about us in the first place, and we wouldn't need to leave."

Mariette raised her chin. "I will tell my story. It's mine to tell, and nothing any of you say or do will stop me."

As much as Thomas admired his grandmother's grit, he was not at all pleased with the dark expressions on the faces of the men at the table. Though Teddy and Cecil weren't young anymore, Thomas knew enough about their history to believe his grandmother was playing with fire. He'd be glad to see the group leave in the morning. *Let them all combust elsewhere.*

Cecil and Teddy left the table and much of the dark cloud in the room left with them. Jacqueline stayed for dessert, a truly amazing crème brûlée. The complex flavor of the caramelized sugar topping married perfectly with the smooth vanilla custard underneath. Still, Thomas ate little of his, as his attention lingered on his grandmother and his worry over her.

As soon as her ramekin was empty, Jacqueline stood and peered down her nose at Mariette. "You ruin everything," she said. "You always have."

Mariette simply waved a languid hand at Jacqueline, which sent the other woman storming from the room.

"You really shouldn't work people up," Thomas said as soon as Jacqueline was out of earshot.

"Jacqueline was born worked up," Mariette said airily.

"It's not Jacqueline who worries me." Thomas dabbed at his mouth, set his napkin aside, and rose. "Please, promise me that you'll stay in your room once you retire. I know you like to wander the halls, but I don't think tonight is a good time for that, and I'll sleep better if I know you're safely behind a locked door."

"You fuss too much."

"And you are entirely too happy poking hornets' nests," Thomas said. "Please promise me."

"I promise," Mariette said. "And I believe I will go to my room now. This business with Matthew has wrung me out. My poor, dear friend."

"Do you have any idea who might want to hurt your friend?" Poppy asked, surprising Thomas. She'd been quiet during dinner, and with all the drama, she'd nearly slipped from his mind.

"I do not," Mariette said and her voice sounded as tired as she'd claimed. "Matthew was truly the best of us. I will miss him terribly."

"I'm sorry for your loss," Poppy said.

Mariette peered at her for a moment, then said, "You know, I believe you are. Good night, dear. We'll begin work in the morning."

"I'll be ready."

After the extremely strange day before, Poppy woke unsure of what to expect from her new project. She wasn't sure how she felt about Teddy, Cecil, and Jacqueline's plans to leave. Normally she would be eager for the material she might glean from any potential drama. But something about getting news of a murder made Poppy unusually reluctant to be around such charismatic people.

She padded across her large room and into the bathroom. It was bigger than the one in her apartment and far more charming, with its claw-foot tub and pretty, barely-blue tiles. She had enjoyed a long soak in the tub before retiring the previous night, so she settled for splashing water on her face as she wanted to get down to breakfast before Mariette's friends left.

At least her relationship with Thomas had smoothed out after its explosive start. She felt a fresh pang of embarrassment at how much she'd misunderstood the situation. "Can't change the past," she reminded her reflection in the antique mirror over the sink.

Poppy dressed quickly in a cozy sweater and lined wool slacks. She'd discovered the heat in the house was uneven. The burst of warmth in the front entry had been like a toasty hug when she'd come in from outside, but since then, she'd discovered more than one of the rooms she'd passed through was almost drafty. Still, it was nothing the right outfit wouldn't fix. As neat and professional as she could manage, she headed down to breakfast, and the excitement started the second she walked into the breakfast room where Thomas and Mariette stood together inside.

"That won't go over well," Thomas was saying.

"What won't?" Poppy asked, hoping neither he nor his grandmother would think her nosy.

Mariette focused on her. "The ferryman flatly refuses to come to the island. It started to snow in the night, and the weather has been getting worse ever since." She waved a hand toward the bank of tall windows.

The view through them was obscured by rough snow, and with her attention on it, Poppy could hear the rattle of icy precipitation being blown against the glass panels.

"The ferryman is right," Thomas said. "This is no weather to be on the water in, no matter how experienced the captain may be."

"Teddy and Cecil will simply have to get over themselves," Mariette said, and Poppy could see the hint of a smile on Mariette's lined face. Poppy's boss was clearly pleased that her guests couldn't leave.

On the other hand, Poppy saw the opposite expression in Thomas's features. "I don't think either Teddy or Cecil is particularly patient or agreeable," he said. "The blizzard could be the mildest storm we're in for."

"Then we shall have to be brave," Mariette said, still smiling.

"Is there any word on how long the bad weather will last?" Poppy asked.

Thomas shook his head. "New England winter is unpredictable at the best of times, and I don't believe this storm will be the best of times."

"We'll be fine here," Mariette said. "This could be fun."

"I seriously doubt that," Thomas said. And Poppy suspected time would prove him right.

Cecil and Teddy walked into the room together. Cecil already had his heavy coat slung over one arm. "Do we have time to eat before the ferry arrives?" he asked. "I hope you told the man to come quickly. The weather is worsening."

"I told him," Mariette said. "For all the good it did. Cass refuses to come."

Cecil's demeanor fairly crackled with annoyance. "He's probably holding out for more money."

"I offered it to him," Mariette assured the tall man. "And he said his life is worth more than whatever I could come up with. I didn't bother to disagree."

"This won't do," Cecil said. "I suppose I can take your boat. You said you have one, right?"

"I did say that because I do," Mariette said hesitantly. "It launches from a different spot than the ferry dock. I keep it in a boathouse to protect it from the vagaries of the weather here. But it's not nearly as large as Cass's fishing boat and is not made for this kind of weather."

"I'm not sure I believe you," Cecil said. "You don't want me to use your boat because you don't want us to leave."

"Of course I don't," Mariette said. "I wouldn't have invited you if I didn't want you here, but the issue truly is the weather. Our boat isn't safe in a storm. I wouldn't go out in it, and none of my staff or family will either."

"I can pilot it," Teddy said. "I've sailed boats in rough weather before."

Cecil cut his eyes toward Teddy. "I will pilot the boat. I'd prefer not to put my life in your hands."

Teddy muttered something under his breath. Poppy didn't quite catch it, but she got the impression it was rude.

Poppy expected Mariette to refuse to let Teddy or Cecil take her boat, especially if it was truly dangerous. Instead, Mariette shrugged elegantly, a bare shift of one shoulder. "Suit yourselves."

"Jackie will need to hear about the change of plans," Teddy said.

Cecil huffed. "You know she hates being called that."

"Not from me," Teddy said with a broad grin.

If he was suggesting some kind of romantic relationship between himself and Jacqueline, Poppy had seen no other sign of it. The actress had shown far more interest in Cecil. The relationships between her fellow guests spun quite a web.

Mariette's light laugh drew Poppy's attention. "I'll be happy to tell Jacqueline whenever the diva drags herself out of bed. Which you both know is going to be noon or later. She's always loved her creature comforts."

Cecil scanned the room as if seeking someone to dump his ire on. Apparently finding no one, he focused on Mariette. "Someone needs to go and rouse her," he said. "Otherwise, I will simply leave her behind."

"I can get her," Teddy said.

Cecil actually chuckled. "She won't be happy about it. You know how much she hates being seen without time to layer on her face." He flicked his finger at Poppy. "You're Mariette's employee. You go and get Jacqueline."

Poppy was startled at the man's casual assumption that he could order her around.

"Poppy isn't a maid," Thomas replied, before she could speak. "And you're not in a position to give orders around here. This is my grandmother's home."

"I don't mind waking Jacqueline," Poppy said, hoping to head off the two men locking horns over a fairly minor breach of good manners. "Her room is across the hall from mine. I'll go check on her."

She hurried out of the room before either man could respond. She hoped a nice breakfast would help everyone to think more clearly and that no one would go out on the water until the storm passed.

She reached Jacqueline's door and saw that it was slightly ajar. She tapped on the door. When no one responded, she knocked more aggressively before peeking in. "Miss Lamarr?" she called. A glance showed her that the room was empty and the bed still made, though it was scattered with discarded clothes.

Poppy wondered where Jacqueline might be. *What's my next move?* She could go tell the moody breakfast bunch that she wasn't able to find Jacqueline, but doubted either Cecil or Teddy would respond well to that. Maybe Poppy should expand her search for the woman.

Jacqueline had struck Poppy as the sort who'd want to poke around in the grand house and discover all its secrets, which was a trait Poppy shared.

So she began her search, moving from room to room and opening doors along the second-floor hall. She met no one, so she headed downstairs. When she reached the bottom of the steps, Poppy walked through a large sitting room and a beautiful library. Neither held Jacqueline.

Finally, Poppy came to a set of closed french doors. Through the glass panels, Poppy could see they didn't lead outside but instead to a large, empty room whose many windows made it plain that the storm was definitely not dying down.

But it wasn't the raging storm that caught and held Poppy's attention.

It was the body sprawled on the floor.

With a yelp, Poppy flung open the door and rushed inside, then dropped to her knees beside the sprawled figure. Though she reached out to touch the ice-cold neck, instinctively checking for a pulse, Poppy had already known she wouldn't find one.

Jacqueline wasn't playacting some dramatic swoon.

She was dead.

Staring down at the phone in his hand, Thomas marveled at how quickly things had spiraled out of control. His grandmother had impulsively decided to invite to her home all the people who would hate her new memoir, and two of them had died. Matthew had never made the trip at all, and Jacqueline met her fate less than a day after arriving on the island. *Dealing with one body will be complicated enough. At least I don't have to handle Matthew's as well.*

He winced at his own callousness. After all, regardless of how little affection he had held for her, a woman was dead.

The police investigator's voice crackled over a wobbly phone connection. "Did you touch the body?"

"I did not," Thomas said. "The young woman who found Jacqueline checked for a pulse. Otherwise, she did not touch the body either."

"Any guess how she died?"

"No," Thomas admitted. "We can't see any sign of violence, so it could have been natural causes. Jacqueline Lamarr is—was in her late seventies, though I'm not privy to her medical history. She was not ill at dinner, but that doesn't mean she didn't grow ill in the night."

"You said the body is in a conservatory," the policeman said. "Is it cold in the room, or can it be made cold?"

"It's cold. Not quite as bad as outside, but possibly near freezing with the storm raging."

"In that case, leave the body in place. Let no one near it. We will not be able to reach you during this storm. It's not safe. We'll be there as soon as the worst of it passes and the crossing can be made safely."

"I understand."

The call ended abruptly. Thomas wasn't certain if the investigator had ended their connection or if his phone had simply lost the signal. He could see one bar flickering at the top of his screen.

"They aren't going to do anything?" Teddy demanded. "What are we supposed to do?"

Thomas slid his phone into his blazer pocket. "There is no access to this island in the storm. No one—not even the police—wants to die attempting to collect a body. It appears we will have to wait until the bad weather passes."

"Poor Jacqueline," Poppy said. "I hate the thought of leaving her in there on the floor. It feels disrespectful." Her voice lacked much of the energy Thomas had noted in his other conversations with her. She was still pale from discovering a dead woman, though he noticed Poppy hadn't let her shock keep her from comforting Mariette.

"I agree," Thomas said. "But we don't have much of a choice." He hated that the horrible weekend had landed on Poppy, but more and more, he was glad she was there. She was a breath of sanity in the chaos.

"We do have choices," Cecil said. "We may not be able to help Jacqueline, but we don't have to remain on the island. There's still Mariette's boat."

"I am certain the police will take an extremely dim view of anyone trying to leave the island before they get here," Thomas said. "Plus, if the weather is too rough for a police boat to reach us, then it's too rough to try taking my grandmother's small boat to the mainland before the blizzard is over."

Cecil's attention sharpened, and he took a single step toward Mariette. "Does this mean you are no longer offering the use of your boat?"

"I don't care if you take the boat," Mariette told him. "It's insured. But you'd better hope Jacqueline's passing was a result of some natural cause, because otherwise the police will consider both of you fleeing suspects. And they do *so* enjoy chasing people who run."

"I haven't decided what I will do," Cecil replied, "but I am not afraid of the police."

"Me neither," Teddy said, though he sounded less certain.

Cecil left the dining room. Teddy tromped after him. His anger and frustration were far easier to read, as was his natural deference to Cecil's decision.

Once the two men were out of the room, Mariette cleared her throat and spoke firmly. "I want to know how Jacqueline died. I believe we should examine her body."

"That is exactly the opposite of what the police instructed," Thomas pointed out. "Determining cause of death is a medical examiner's job. Staying away from the body is our job. We need to keep everyone out of there. Does the conservatory even lock?"

"No," Mariette said. "Though Arthur may have some idea as to how to secure the door. But I really must insist we check for signs of murder first. I don't want to be trapped in here with a killer unawares."

"When I went to check after Poppy alerted us, I saw no sign of violence," Thomas said. "But I did not touch the body."

"I did," Poppy said. "She was cold and stiff. I'm not an expert, but I imagine it would have taken time for her to get so cold. Hours at least."

"Poor Jacqueline," Mariette murmured, for the first time sounding as caring as Poppy. "So you don't think she was murdered?"

Poppy didn't answer at once. When she did, her tone was careful. "Jacqueline's position hid her face and the front of her body. But if she were walking around in the night and simply got dizzy and fell, I think she would have died of hypothermia in that room eventually. She wasn't dressed for the temperature in the conservatory."

Mariette nodded, then raised her chin. "Understood. I still want to see her." She brushed past Thomas and headed out the doorway.

Poppy followed her, and Thomas hurried to catch up. "Surely you don't think this is a good idea," he said to Poppy. "Defying police instruction."

"I think Mariette is going to do whatever she pleases," Poppy said. "And I'm not happy with the possibility, however slight it may be, that someone might have killed Jacqueline. Based on that possibility, I'm not letting your grandmother go to the conservatory alone."

"Good girl," Mariette called over her shoulder, never slowing.

Thomas didn't bother arguing, knowing a lost cause when he saw one. "Are you really worried that Jacqueline was murdered? I thought you said you didn't see any evidence of that."

"I didn't," Poppy said. "But I'm not a coroner or a medical examiner. I'm a ghostwriter who saw my first dead body today, and hopefully my last."

"Even without wounds," Mariette said, slowing slightly to let them catch up, "Jacqueline could have been poisoned."

"Poisoned? Really?" Thomas asked. "We're not in the middle of a Gothic novel." He noticed Poppy shudder beside him. "What?"

"Nothing. Your comment reminded me of something I thought about earlier. I was marveling at how this house could have come from one of the English Gothic novels I read when I was younger."

Mariette clapped her hands lightly. "A Gothic novel. Maybe that's exactly where we are."

"We're in the middle of a New England snowstorm," Thomas said, "not the British moors."

"Where's your imagination?" his grandmother asked him. Then they passed through the last doorway to the short hall outside the conservatory. Mariette didn't even pause, but boldly threw open the doors and walked through. Once more, they were met with an icy chill and the sight of the storm raging against all the windows in the room.

Mariette paused beside Jacqueline's body and bent over to see her friend better.

"Don't touch her," Thomas called out, hoping to preserve some element of the police detective's order.

Mariette didn't respond, merely leaning slightly to see the body at a new angle. As he watched his grandmother, he was struck by how physically similar Jacqueline and Mariette were. The white-blonde wig that Jacqueline wore, slightly askew, must have looked identical to Mariette's hair in the dark. Jacqueline had gone to great lengths to copy Mariette, but many of their similarities in build and height were natural.

Thomas felt a pang of fear. He hoped desperately that Jacqueline's death had been natural, because he suddenly had the horrible realization that, if Jacqueline was murdered, she might not have been the intended victim. Mariette was known to suffer from insomnia and meander in the night. If Jacqueline had been similarly wandering around the house in the dark, a killer could easily have mistaken the actress for Mariette. And if that were the case, the killer might not be finished.

The frigid chill in the conservatory sank into Poppy's core, and she hugged herself in an effort to stave off shivering. She couldn't take her eyes off the shockingly still figure on the cracked stone floor.

Jacqueline was in exactly the same position as she had been when Poppy found her, and, though much of the shock of seeing her had worn off, the sadness remained. Jacqueline hadn't been a particularly pleasant woman, but she'd been a human being, and her life was suddenly over.

Dragging her attention away from Jacqueline, Poppy redirected it toward the nearest window, where the storm made the view as dull and dark as evening despite it being barely past breakfast time. *What a desolate and lonely place to die.*

"Roll the body over." Mariette's demand made Poppy gape. Did she care nothing about what the police had ordered?

Poppy returned her focus to the body as Thomas argued with his grandmother, reminding her that the police wouldn't appreciate their choice to completely ignore instruction. Poppy spotted something she hadn't noticed before. "Wait." She edged closer and knelt beside the body again, while a part of her recoiled from what she was about to do. She reached out a hand.

"We're not supposed to touch her," Thomas said.

"I already have," Poppy said. "So no one new needs to get in trouble if I touch her again." She ran her fingers lightly over Jacqueline's head where she'd noticed an odd shadowing on the wig the older woman wore. Under the wig, she felt a definite indentation where one should not be. The wig had made it difficult to see, but even so, she knew that something wasn't quite right.

Poppy raised her eyes, meeting Mariette's curious gaze, and Thomas's annoyed one. "I think her skull has been damaged. I can feel a rough impression. The wig is hiding how bad the damage is. I suspect the wound would be obvious if we took the wig off."

"So take it off," Mariette said.

"No," Thomas replied forcefully. He'd been pushed far enough, and Poppy suspected they would meet real resistance if they pressed him any farther.

His grandmother continued anyway. "If someone struck Jacqueline and killed her, I want to know."

"Seeing blood won't tell you anything Poppy hasn't already said," Thomas insisted. "And I'd prefer to adhere to the police directions as much as possible. If we want law enforcement to find the killer, we need to avoid interfering with evidence. If Poppy says Jacqueline's head is damaged, I believe her."

"Jacqueline was murdered," Mariette said, her voice sounding almost forlorn. "Two of my oldest friends have been killed."

Poppy rose to her feet. "We don't yet know for sure that she was murdered. Jacqueline isn't far from the stone bench there. If she was wandering around last night, she was doing so in the dark. She could have come in here and tripped. The floor is broken in places, and there's debris here and there. If Jacqueline fell against that bench, it could have caused the damage I felt."

"She's close to it, but not that close," Mariette said. "How did she get here?"

"Head injuries don't always cause immediate death," Poppy said. "She may have crawled this far, or even gotten up, walked a few steps, and fallen again."

"The police can tell us when they get here," Thomas said, his tone firm. "Though I am troubled by the apparent coincidence of Jacqueline dying from a blow to the head so shortly after Matthew was murdered. I don't suppose the police said anything about Matthew receiving a head injury?"

"They weren't so forthcoming," Mariette explained. "I imagine we'll hear more from them about Matthew eventually. I hate waiting around. I am not used to feeling so helpless."

"There are several things about this situation that worry me," Thomas said. "Foremost being the possibility that you are in danger and so is Poppy."

"What a preposterous idea," Mariette said. "Why would anyone bother killing me? I'm dying anyway, Thomas. They could simply wait out my fate. Besides, these people and I may have been influential in our day, but that time has long since passed."

"And yet, Jacqueline is dead. Matthew is dead. And I am troubled by how much Jacqueline resembled you." Thomas shook his head as if he found it hard to believe his own words. "With your habit of wandering the house at night, anyone who came across Jacqueline in the dark could easily have mistaken her for you. Which makes me worry about the intentions someone has for you if they did this to Jacqueline, thinking she was you."

Mariette absorbed the information in silence, but the change in her expression was obvious. Her defiance washed away. "You think I was the intended victim?"

"I can't know for certain," Thomas said. "But I think we have to consider it as a possibility."

"We don't really know what's going on," Poppy said. "Thomas wants us to be careful, that's all. And maybe we could start by relocating to a room where we won't all freeze to death?"

"Of course." Thomas herded them toward the door. "I think neither of you should wander around alone. And when you're in your rooms, I believe you should lock your doors."

"I will," Mariette said. "if you promise to stop nagging. I will travel with Poppy, and we will guard one another." She linked her arm with Poppy's and they walked out into the warmer hallway. "We have a lot of work to do anyway. We can push some of this horror out of our minds by starting on the book."

Poppy could tell by Thomas's face that he thought Mariette's plan was terrible, but he didn't comment. He was probably relieved that his grandmother was making some effort to comply with reason.

While they were still in the hall, Arthur appeared, striding toward them with a vigor Poppy would have expected from a younger man.

"You should have called me," the butler said. "I heard about the murder from Mrs. Bing."

"You have breakfast hours off," Mariette said. "I saw no reason to hurry you. It would make poor Jacqueline no less dead. But now that you're here, we need some way to secure the conservatory so our guests can't wander into it."

Arthur eyed the french doors. "I have some chain and a lock. I purchased it to use on the boathouse when we changed the lock over the summer. It should secure the room if I loop the chain over the handles and padlock them."

Mariette patted the big man's arm. "I knew you'd figure it out. Please do that as soon as you can. Now, Poppy and I are going to the study. Thomas, help Arthur if he needs it."

"I cannot imagine Arthur needs help with a lock and chain," Thomas said. "I will join you in the study."

Poppy wasn't sure how she felt about the idea of Thomas hanging around while they worked. She liked him and was starting to hope Mariette's grandson might become a friend, but he brought out the stubborn side of his grandmother, and that wouldn't necessarily be helpful.

As they walked down the corridor, Poppy tried to think of a diplomatic way to suggest Thomas should find a better use of his time, but she hadn't come up with anything when they reached the bottom of the wide staircase.

But it didn't matter, because they were suddenly frozen in their tracks by a high, piercing scream.

$\mathcal{W}$ithout a second thought, Poppy launched herself up the stairs toward the scream. She heard Thomas call after her, but she didn't respond. She knew Mariette couldn't possibly run up the stairs, and she would rather Thomas stayed with his grandmother and kept her safe anyway.

On the second floor, she turned away from the hall that led to her room and raced down the opposite corridor where Mrs. Bing stood at an open doorway, hands pressed to her chest. The housekeeper was staring into a room as Poppy reached her and laid a gentle hand on her arm.

Mrs. Bing jumped and recoiled away from Poppy, her eyes wide with shock and fear.

"What's wrong?" Poppy asked, though she was already leaning around to peer through the doorway for herself.

"In there." Mrs. Bing gaped at the open door. "Dead."

Poppy eased around the housekeeper and walked into the room. It was as large as the one Poppy had, though not as bright. The walls were wood-clad, and the color scheme was darker, favoring maroons and grays. Poppy barely noticed though, as her attention was mainly on the sprawling body of Teddy Marcone.

Though terrified that she'd found another dead body, Poppy knelt immediately. Once she was close to Teddy, the rise and fall of his chest was obvious. She pressed her fingers to his neck and found a strong pulse.

"What happened?" Mariette had reached the second floor, though she was still at the top of the landing. Her imperious tone was slightly breathy, and Thomas was close by her side.

Mrs. Bing didn't even try to speak again and only pointed a shaking hand toward the empty room.

"How is he?" Thomas asked, and Poppy shifted position to face him, but not much as she kept her fingers on Teddy's neck.

"His pulse is strong. We should elevate his feet, I think." Poppy had taken a first aid course as a teenager, so her memory of what to do for an unconscious person was slightly vague, but she remembered something about keeping the feet above the head. But then she also remembered something about a rescue position and knew she was way out of her depth. "I wish we could call 911."

"We could call," Thomas said as he grabbed a small, low footstool and shoved it under Teddy's feet. "They couldn't come, but we could call."

"And to think I was looking forward to how exciting this weekend would be," Poppy muttered before leaning close and patting Teddy's cheeks while calling out, "Mr. Marcone? Can you hear me?"

Teddy's eyes fluttered in response to her voice. She rubbed his hand, then patted his face again, still calling his name. Eventually his eyes opened and stayed open.

"What happened?" he asked, his dark eyes troubled.

"I was hoping you could tell us," Thomas said.

"Mrs. Bing found you on the floor," Poppy added.

"You scared the poor woman half to death," Mariette added from the doorway.

"Oh," Teddy said. His face had been pale when Poppy first knelt beside him, but his color was quickly returning to normal. "Can you help me sit up?"

"Okay," Poppy said, "But if you feel dizzy, let me know right away."

"I will."

With Thomas's help, they hauled Teddy to a sitting position. "What happened?" Thomas asked. "Do you remember?"

Teddy shook his head. "I have a history of orthostatic hypotension."

"What on earth does that mean?" Mariette demanded.

"Sudden drops in blood pressure," Poppy answered. Since Teddy had named it, she was mildly surprised she hadn't thought of it immediately. Her grandmother had suffered from the same problem and had to wear expensive compression socks, and even compression sleeves when the condition worsened. "Do you not have compression socks?"

Teddy harrumphed. "My doctor told me to get them, but I'm not about to parade around in compression socks. Those are for old ladies."

Mariette snorted. "How clever of you. Fainting on your bedroom floor is quite preferable to wearing medical socks."

The expression Teddy aimed in her direction at the comment was positively chilling, and Poppy worried that it wasn't wise for Mariette to goad the man. He had a medical condition, but he was still an imposing man with a bad temper.

"You always did have a way with words," Teddy said, his eyes still on Mariette. "I never understood how Joseph tolerated it."

"Joseph loved me," Mariette said. "Something you couldn't possibly understand." She raised her chin. "Come along, Poppy. If Teddy isn't interested in taking proper care of himself, that's his prerogative. We have work to do. Thomas can wrestle Teddy into a chair."

"I can help," Poppy said to Thomas. She was beginning to suspect it wouldn't be a good idea to let Mariette get used to ordering her around.

As Poppy and Thomas helped Teddy into a chair, Mariette waited impatiently in the hall, something she apparently didn't enjoy. "Mrs. Bing," Mariette said sharply. "I'll thank you to limit your screaming to actual dead bodies in the future. It's quite disruptive to get everyone upset over nothing."

All of a sudden, Poppy realized that not everyone appeared to be upset. Where was Cecil? Why hadn't he responded to Mrs. Bing's screaming? Poppy assumed that anyone who'd heard the shrieks would wonder what happened and want to investigate. So why wasn't Cecil there, throwing insults at Teddy?

Poppy put her face close to Thomas's ear. "Why isn't Cecil here?"

Surprise bloomed on Thomas's face, and his gaze flicked to the hallway, where only Mrs. Bing and Mariette stood. "An excellent question. I'll find out." He jerked his head toward the doorway. "Don't leave my grandmother alone, please."

"I won't," Poppy assured him. She didn't blame him for being worried. She was worried as well.

"Come along, Poppy," Mariette called from the hallway. "Thomas can take care of Teddy now. I want to get to work."

"Of course," Poppy said, heading toward the door.

Thomas caught her arm. "Be careful."

She nodded, and he released her. She trotted quickly out into the hall, giving herself the luxury of a glance behind her. She wished she could go with Thomas as he searched for Cecil, since she couldn't shake the worry that her remark about Cecil may have sent Thomas into something dangerous. If something happened to him, it would be her fault.

Teddy's color had completely returned to normal, and the man demanded that Thomas leave him alone and stop fussing.

"No problem," Thomas said, heading gladly out of the room.

A Chilling Reunion 65

Mrs. Bing still stood in the hall. She wasn't quite as pale, but her eyes were slightly unfocused, and she twisted her fingers together.

Thomas stopped at her side. "You should take a break. Go down and have a cup of tea."

"I'm sorry I screamed, sir," the woman said quietly.

"Don't give it a thought. We're all on edge. Please take a quiet moment to yourself."

"Thank you, sir." The housekeeper gave Teddy's room one last glance and shuddered, then hurried away.

"Close that door," Teddy ordered. "I've been gawked at enough."

Thomas took hold of the doorknob, then paused to ask, "Any idea where Cecil is?"

"I haven't seen him. Last interaction we had was when I told him we should wait until the storm let up to take the boat and leave."

"He wasn't a fan of the idea?"

"Cecil has never been a fan of being questioned." Teddy relaxed in the chair and closed his eyes. "Don't forget to close the door."

Thomas closed it. He headed down the hall to Cecil's room and rapped on the door. There was no answer. He opened it and peered in. The room was quiet and empty.

"He must be outside," Thomas concluded. He could keep searching the house, of course, but somehow he was certain Cecil had gone to the boathouse.

He trotted down the steps and went in search of Arthur, who was attaching the lock to the conservatory door. "I found a tablecloth," Arthur said as Thomas walked up. "Never out of the package. I used it to cover Miss Lamarr. I imagine the police won't approve of it, but once upon a time I loved the woman's movies, and I suppose I couldn't bear the indignity. Who knows how long this storm will last?"

Thomas wished Arthur hadn't gone into the conservatory. The police wouldn't appreciate hearing how much the crime scene traffic had increased from what he'd initially reported, but there was no point scolding Arthur after the fact. "That was kind of you. Did you hear Mrs. Bing scream?"

Arthur blinked in surprise. "No. Is she hurt?"

"No, she misunderstood something she'd seen. She's fine." But Arthur's reaction meant the scream hadn't carried as far as he'd expected. Maybe Cecil had not heard it either. "Have you seen Cecil Lewis this morning?"

"I passed him earlier in the front entryway," Arthur said. "He was putting on his heavy coat, so I assume he went outside. I recommended against it, and he reminded me I was a butler and should mind my own business." He recited the encounter without emotion.

"Your recommendation was spot-on," Thomas said. "Unfortunately now I need to go outside as well. I have to make sure Cecil isn't out there collapsed on a rock somewhere."

"Do you want me to go with you?"

Thomas suppressed a smile. Arthur took his responsibilities seriously. "That's not necessary. Could you make sure my grandmother and Poppy get safely to the study? If you could keep an eye on them while I'm outside, I'd appreciate it."

"Of course." Arthur tipped his head.

As reluctant as Thomas was to go outside in the weather, he knew it would be worse to put it off. He did allow himself the tiny hope that the front door would open and Cecil would come in while Thomas was putting on his coat, scarf, and knit hat? That didn't happen, so Thomas finally unlocked the front door and opened it, pushing hard against the heavy wood to fight the wind that was determined to keep the door closed.

Once outside, the rough wind threw icy crystals into Thomas's eyes, making them sting and burn. He squinted, peering around him through bare slits. He wondered how Cecil would even know where the family boathouse was. He didn't remember Mariette giving out any explicit directions, and Arthur hadn't mentioned being questioned. Maybe he'd ask Cecil when he found him.

Thomas turned up his coat collar and pulled his scarf tighter, then set off into the storm. He was grateful for the well-worn path to the boathouse. With the blowing storm, sometimes Thomas walked on a completely clear path, the wind not allowing the snow to settle, then he'd hit another place where sheltering trees blocked the wind and the path vanished under the snow, forcing him to guess at the right direction.

Each time he found the walkway again, he was flooded with fresh relief. The buffeting wind made him stagger, and every step took focused effort. Thomas asked himself repeatedly if he shouldn't simply quit, go back to the warm, dry house, and leave Cecil to whatever consequences his stupid choices had created. But Thomas knew his grandmother would be disappointed in him if he did, so he pressed on.

Thomas had always enjoyed snow in New England, when it floated gently down like feathers. The current storm was neither gentle nor beautiful. The snowfall consisted of hard, sharp pellets that the wind flung roughly against the windows and walls of the house, and against him. Visibility was near zero and the island was dim, even though it was long past sunrise. Up ahead on the path, trees would appear and disappear in the sheeting snow, and Thomas had to count on the feel of the worn path under his boots as much as any visual cues.

The path curved, sloping slowly downward, but never steeply. Still, even the slight angle was enough to make the snow-covered spots slippery, and Thomas was grateful for his expensive boots and their gripping tread, designed especially for such conditions.

After a long, miserable trudge, Thomas finally saw the ghost of the boathouse perched at the edge of the water. He'd made it. He wrenched open the boathouse door and staggered inside where Cecil stood, arms wrapped around his chest. "Thomas," Cecil said by way of greeting.

"You need to come with me," Thomas said. "You have to realize that taking the boat out in this would be suicidal."

"That won't be a problem," Cecil said. "I'm not taking the boat."

"Good," Thomas said, but something in Cecil's tone suggested otherwise.

"Not really."

"What do you mean?"

Cecil gestured toward the boat. "See for yourself."

The boat sat low in the water, far lower than it should. As Thomas stepped closer to the vessel, he realized the hull must have been resting on the bottom in the shallow water of the boathouse. "What?"

"There's a hole," Cecil said. "You can see it if you move further toward the prow."

Thomas followed Cecil's direction and saw the rough hole, barely visible below the water. Cecil was right about no one taking the boat anywhere.

Someone had bashed a hole in it.

Though she prided herself on being professional even under stress, Poppy had to admit that Mariette did not have her full attention as they sat in the cozy study with the sound of a crackling fire almost drowned out by occasional howls of wind. Part of her listened for Thomas's return and worried the longer she didn't hear it. Poppy told herself that she simply didn't want anything else horrible to happen, and that was true enough, but she also knew her concern for Thomas might have been slightly more personal.

You barely know that man, she scolded herself inwardly.

"Poppy," Mariette said. "Are you with me?"

Poppy managed not to jump as her boss's voice cut into her musing, but she felt her face warm nonetheless. "Yes ma'am."

Mariette groaned. "Don't 'ma'am' me, please. I don't blame you for checking out. I wish as much as you do that Thomas and Cecil weren't outside."

"They strike me as capable men," Poppy said.

"That they are. But it doesn't mean I don't worry." Mariette settled deeper into her chair. "I know you weren't around Cass for long, but I'm sure that rascal told you that I am cursed. It's a theory he enjoys."

"I have a policy of not listening to nonsense," Poppy said.

Mariette laughed. "My dear, you should *always* listen to nonsense. That's where all the most interesting things lie. And who knows? I may be cursed. I'm not proud of my life—not really. I've sometimes been cruel, and far too often I was oblivious to what my husband and Cecil were doing."

Poppy raised her eyebrows. "Illegal things?"

"Undoubtedly," Mariette said. "But none of us worried much about the law. It was there to be managed, not obeyed, but there are far worse things than breaking the law. My Joseph once bought a chemical company located outside the US. The company apparently produced some extremely effective insecticide, but it couldn't be used in this country because it made people sick."

"That doesn't sound like a good investment," Poppy said.

"You'd think. Joseph said the US laws were too strict, and companies were suffering losses due to pests. I believe that pesticide *was* used, despite the law. I never asked too many questions about it—which I regret—but I really should have known Joseph wouldn't miss out on a profit in the end."

"So you don't know if anyone was hurt," Poppy said carefully.

Mariette shook her head. "No, and to my shame, I didn't try to find out. I didn't ask. I didn't dig into the affairs of my husband and his company, then or at any other time. And now I can't even count the costs, because I never made an effort to notice them. Even now, I'm afraid to dig into it."

"I could try to find out if you want," Poppy said. "There might be people you could help, people who were affected by those choices with whom you could try to make reparations."

Mariette didn't answer at once, and Poppy waited patiently while the older woman thought it through. "Yes. Perhaps you could do that. I would like to help those people."

Poppy shifted in her seat as her brain changed gears. "I know Cecil was your husband's business partner. But I don't know how Teddy or Jacqueline figure in. Or Matthew Bellamy, for that matter. Was he a business partner too?"

"On paper, yes," Mariette said. "Matthew was Joseph's oldest friend.

They'd known each other since they were boys. And Matthew always served as Joseph's conscience. He had such a core of fairness and kindness."

"So how did he feel about your husband's business practices?"

"Matthew tried to be the conscience of the business, as he had always been Joseph's conscience throughout their friendship. But business is far harder to restrain, and business acumen wasn't Matthew's gift the way it was Joseph's. My husband could see how different things fit together to produce obscene profits, and he made it happen over and over. Matthew came to hate what the business was doing. Ultimately, it was Matthew who came to me and tried to make me see the damage being done in my name as much as Joseph's."

"And then?" Poppy asked when Mariette stopped talking, her expression troubled.

"I wouldn't listen. You have to understand that I was besotted with my husband. And he was a good husband. He loved me, and he loved our daughter. In the face of that, it was hard to see business as anything other than an abstract thing, far removed from me."

"What's different now?"

"After Joseph died, Matthew and I were close for a while. He is a caring person. But he wanted to make the wrongs of the past public. He was already pressing for some kind of restitution for anyone hurt by decisions the business made. I wanted to make restitution and would have been happy for Matthew to simply track those people down so I could authorize an agreed-upon amount. But I wanted it quiet. I didn't want to drag my husband's name through public censure."

"I can understand why you feel that way," Poppy said.

"Can you?" Mariette's tone was forlorn. "I can't excuse it, not completely. Some of my protectiveness was on account of my daughter. She adored her father, and seeing that side of him would have hurt her terribly. But still, staying quiet simply kept the wrongdoing covered up.

Matthew left the final decision to me, and that's what I chose. But the idea has stayed in my head."

"You're planning to write your memoir now," Poppy said. "Does that mean your views have changed?"

"Some." Mariette's eyes were bright with unshed tears, though her voice remained clear. "Matthew was so happy when I called to tell him that the time had arrived for the truth to come out. I said I would reveal everything in my memoir. And he could do the same if he wanted. He was so eager to be here, eager to help and support me. That's why I was surprised when he wasn't on the boat with you and the others." Her voice broke, and her next words were so quiet Poppy had to lean close to hear them. "And now he's gone. I can hardly believe it."

Poppy wondered if Matthew's death had anything to do with the secrets they planned to reveal together. If he'd begun uncovering things immediately, it could be that he'd upset someone who wasn't ready for the truth to come out.

"I still don't know how Teddy and Jacqueline fit into all of this," Poppy said.

"Teddy worked for Joseph and Cecil sometimes," Mariette said. "He was on the books as a consultant, but I cannot imagine what sorts of things Teddy would consult on. He was never as bright as either Joseph or Cecil, but he's sly."

"From my reading, I had the impression he was connected with organized crime."

"How diplomatic you are. Yes, Teddy was connected in all sorts of ways. But now he's an old man. We're all old, and our connections are far weaker than they once were."

Poppy wasn't at all sure that meant Teddy and Cecil were harmless. *An old cobra will strike slower, but you're equally dead if it bites you.* "And Jacqueline?"

"Poor Jacqueline," Mariette said. "She really was so far from the inner circle, but she longed to be part of it. She dated Teddy at one point, and Cecil at another. I always suspected she was in love with Joseph, but he was in love with me and that never wavered. There are many things my husband was guilty of, but unfaithfulness was not one of them. I invited her because she will be part of my memoirs, tangentially. She was here socially so often."

"I see," Poppy said, though she remained somewhat confounded by all the connections.

"Do you?" Mariette's face fell into weary folds. "Jacqueline wasn't a particularly nice person, but I'm still grieved by her loss. She had her good side. Sometimes I felt that we truly were friends. Not often, but sometimes. And she was surprisingly fond of Bethany."

Poppy knew Bethany was Mariette's daughter, Bethany Nordwich. "I have to admit, my preparatory research found almost nothing about Bethany. Not even a wedding notice."

"Bethany hates being in the public eye. She always did. I think it was that paranoid fear of being observed by strangers that destroyed her marriage, not that she ever told me much about it. We do not get along."

"I got that feeling," Poppy said. "I assume we'll be going into it in the book."

"Perhaps some," Mariette said. She relaxed in her seat, and her gaze drifted toward the fire. In repose, she struck Poppy as tired for the first time. "Mothers and daughters. It can be complicated sometimes."

"And now?"

"My darling Joseph had cancer. Did you know? That's what killed him. He was diagnosed but refused treatment. He hated the idea of what he perceived as weakness. I wanted him to try, but he wouldn't even consider it. Bethany thinks I should have forced him.

She believes I encouraged his stubbornness to rush along his death, but she's wrong. I would have done almost anything to have more days with my beloved."

"Grief can make people irrational," Poppy said.

"Perhaps. It didn't help that Bethany and I were never as close as I would have liked. I thought with time that we could reconcile. That we could talk it out. At the very least, I expected her to show up this weekend to state her displeasure at my memoir."

"She has said she disapproves?"

"Through Thomas. I had hoped her feelings would soften once she learned the news that I am dying, but she's as stubborn as her father—as stubborn as me."

"You don't strike me as ill," Poppy said.

"For now. But even now I am not without pain. I am stubborn, as I said, and you'd be amazed at how much stubbornness can overcome." Mariette took a deep breath, then appeared to shake off some of her melancholy. She beamed at Poppy. "What do you think of my grandson?"

"I think he loves you," Poppy said. She suspected that wasn't what Mariette was fishing for, but she wasn't ready to discuss her budding attraction to Thomas.

"Thomas is a good man," Mariette said.

Poppy realized she wanted to learn more about Mariette's grandson. The conflict between wanting to know more and not wanting to signal the slightest interest held her silent until they heard shouting.

"Where is everyone? We need to talk. Now," a voice called from the hall.

Recognizing Thomas's voice, Poppy was on her feet in an instant. She started toward the door, then spun when she heard her employer moan, "Who's dead now?"

By the time everyone had gathered in the dining room, the warmth of the house had finally begun to seep into Thomas, though he wasn't sure how much longer it would take before he'd feel comfortable. The temperature outside, compounded by the driving snow, was brutal.

"Since everyone is here," Mariette said. "I shall assume there have been no additional deaths. I'll thank you not to scare me that way again, Thomas."

"Fear is an appropriate response to this weekend's events," Thomas said. He scanned the dining room, examining each face and wondering which of the people had bashed a hole in their sole means of escape from the island. He felt sure it wasn't his grandmother. She was making a good show, but he knew she was far weaker than she'd been even a few short weeks ago.

Thomas also couldn't bring himself even to suspect Poppy. He told himself it was because such an act wasn't something of which she seemed capable, rather than that he was starting to feel a spark of attraction to her.

He wasn't so quick to let Cecil off the hook, despite the man's age. Thomas had found him in the boathouse, after all. Cecil had insisted he wanted off the island, but what if that was camouflage for something else? Thomas knew his grandmother's memoir wasn't going to make Cecil happy at all. Thomas studied the older man, sitting easily now. The only signs that he'd been out in severe weather were his damp hair and dark cuffs on his pants where they'd soaked through. Thomas suspected his own cuffs would be similarly wet and dirty, though he couldn't feel the dampness because of the boots he wore.

Teddy was potentially cleared simply because he'd been found unconscious on his floor after breakfast, but what if that was a ruse?

If he'd damaged the boat early in the morning, he could have waited until he knew Cecil would be going out, then set about displaying some weakness that would make him appear too frail to have done the damage. But Thomas couldn't see Teddy as frail.

Thomas forced his attention away from the guests and studied the staff—butler, housekeeper, and cook. Arthur Kent stood between the two women, his stoic face revealing nothing. Mrs. Bing twisted her hands together and cast fearful glances toward the windows where the blizzard raged on. The cook, Maddie Harris, studied the room curiously but showed no sign of distress. Thomas wished bad guys were easier to detect.

He cleared his throat. "Someone doesn't want us to leave this island—that much is clear."

"Is it?" Mariette asked. "There's a storm raging, Thomas. I know the boat is in the boathouse, but the building is old. Isn't it possible the storm damaged the boat?"

"No, it's not," Thomas said flatly. "I saw the hole in the bottom of the boat." He studied the group again, making eye contact with each person before moving on. "And I believe the person who damaged the boat probably murdered Jacqueline as well."

That drew a gasp from Mrs. Bing and a sharp inquisitive expression from the cook, but no one else appeared particularly moved by what Thomas had hoped was a dramatic reveal.

"What makes you think Jacqueline was murdered?" Cecil demanded.

"Yeah," Teddy echoed. "I figured she just up and died. At our age, people do that sometimes."

"I'm not sure that's true, Teddy," Mariette said. "We may not hear what exactly killed people, but I'm quite sure there is no spontaneous death waiting for any of us."

"Life is more mysterious than you know," Teddy said loftily.

"Didn't Shakespeare say that? You know, the heaven-and-earth philosophies thing."

"You really should not talk so much, Teddy," Cecil said. "People are more impressed by the strong, silent type."

Teddy narrowed his eyes at Cecil, obviously not sure how to react to what the other man had said.

"If you'll let me go on," Thomas said. "Jaqueline was wearing a wig when she died, but even without removing it, one can feel that the skull is concave in one area." He didn't bother to say who had felt the skull depression. He didn't want to direct too much attention toward Poppy. "Though it's not definitive. She could, I suppose, have hit her head accidentally somehow, but I'm inclined toward the worst-case scenario, especially when it's coupled with the damaged boat. That boat didn't damage itself."

"I don't suppose it hurts to be careful," Teddy said.

Thomas doubted he'd get anything useful from Teddy or Cecil, so he focused on the three servants. "Did anyone hear or see anything unusual last night?"

"Cook and I don't sleep in the house," Mrs. Bing said. "We have apartments in the old lighthouse keeper's cottage. And we don't wander around much on our way home each night. It's too cold to linger."

That was a surprise to Thomas, though he knew it shouldn't have been. What else had he missed because he paid so little attention to things like the staff's sleeping quarters? "Neither of you left the cottage last night?"

"You can't be serious," Mrs. Bing said. "The walk to the apartment was short, but it took a solid half hour before I warmed up afterward. I had no desire to do it twice." She pivoted to meet the eyes of the cook, who nodded, but Maddie's expression was difficult to read, and Thomas locked onto that.

The cook was older than Mrs. Bing. Thomas would have guessed her to be in her midfifties. The woman had pleasant plump features and an intelligent spark in her eyes under short graying hair.

"Ms. Harris," Thomas said. "Did you see anything in the night?"

"You can call me Cook," the woman said. "Everyone does. As to your question, I'm not sure. I usually sleep like the dead, but the wind was so loud. The snow had started, though it still had a way to go before it hit the worst we've seen so far. It certainly rattled the old windows."

"So you heard the storm." Thomas wondered whether he would have to drag whatever she was trying not to say out of her by inches.

"I did," she said. "I went over to the window in my bedroom. I looked out, mostly to see how much the wind was blowing the trees, but I saw a person. Someone moving around on the path between the cottage and the house." She stopped, and her round cheeks grew pink. "I thought it was a ghost."

"A ghost?" Thomas asked.

"The lighthouse keeper's wife," Cook said. "There's a stupid story about it in the village. Everyone knows it. The first lighthouse keeper brought his young wife to the island so they wouldn't have to be apart so much. But she couldn't stand the loneliness and the cold. She threw herself from the top of the lighthouse. Her ghost is supposed to haunt the island."

"That's ridiculous," Mariette snapped. "There's no such thing as ghosts. I thought you had more sense."

"I do," Cook said, surprising Thomas with her willingness to argue with his grandmother. "I never believed that silly tale, but in the dark and the storm, it sounded much more plausible."

"Excuse me," Arthur cut in. Everyone faced him to find that his normally stalwart countenance was positively sheepish. "I imagine

Cook saw me. I always go out and make sure the two women make it safely to the cottage. I left the house last night to do that."

"We don't need a sitter," Mrs. Bing said with a surprising amount of spirit for someone who'd behaved somewhat meekly thus far.

Arthur didn't bother to argue with her. But Cook spoke up. "What I saw happened hours after we left the house. I was already in bed and got up. And I wasn't dreaming." She addressed the last sentence toward her employer.

"You said you thought it was the ghost from the story," Thomas said. "Does that mean you recognized it as the figure of a woman?"

Cook shook her head. "I don't know. In the storm, all I could tell was that it was human. I couldn't make out any details."

"So it could have simply been your eyes playing tricks with the dark and the storm," Mariette said.

"Maybe it was Jacqueline," Teddy said. "We know she was up."

"It couldn't have been her," Poppy broke in. "We can be sure of that. If she'd been out in the storm, it would have been obvious on her nightgown. Not to mention the fact that she was dressed for bed, not for wandering in a raging blizzard."

Thomas tended to agree with Poppy. Whoever had been out in the snowstorm would show signs of it. He and Cecil had shucked off their coats and scarves, but he could see Cecil's hair was still wet from the melted snow, and he'd noticed moisture on the man's cuffs. Of course, that wouldn't be very helpful. Cook, the housekeeper, the butler, Cecil, and Thomas himself had been out in the snow at different times for various reasons, so wet clothes or dampness might be easily explained.

Still, he hadn't heard a reason why Teddy might have been out of the house, so he suggested, "We should check everyone's clothes. See who shows signs of having gone outside."

"You mean other than you and Cecil," Teddy said. "I went out this morning after arguing with Mariette. I wanted to see exactly how bad the storm was. It's how I decided I did *not* want to take a boat out. I intended to refuse if Cecil went through with the plan, but then I started feeling unwell, so I went up to my room."

"Unless that last part is a lie," Cecil said, "and you went down to the boathouse and bashed in the boat so you didn't have to admit to being a coward who is afraid of the weather."

Teddy's glare was hard and hot. "You push your luck hard sometimes, old friend."

Cecil snorted. "You don't frighten me at all. You never did."

Thomas had no desire to watch the argument escalate into another physical fight between the two. His ribs still ached when he moved, and he wasn't anxious to add to his injuries, especially with a murderer on the loose. "Let's say calm."

"A clothing check is no use," Mariette said. "I'm certain none of my clothes are damp, but I doubt anyone could imagine me braving the elements and bashing in a boat."

"Oh, I don't know," Cecil said. "I can imagine it quite well."

Mariette smiled at him. "Why, what a sweet thing to say."

"I don't mind bringing down my coat if you want to examine it," Poppy said.

"No, that's fine." Thomas was beginning to feel foolish for suggesting it in the first place. The two people he considered valid suspects had excuses for being wet. But Thomas knew that if he couldn't get answers, he'd have to settle for being careful. Because he wasn't certain the danger was over. Not by a long shot.

8

Poppy dropped onto the desk chair in her room. She was exhausted by the stress of the day, though it was barely afternoon. How would she make it through the weekend? "Well, I wanted excitement," she muttered.

Poppy pulled her laptop of out of her bag and began making notes from her session with Mariette. As she typed, she added a few reminders about Mariette's vocal patterns and style, things to keep in mind as she wrote the book. She often made notes about her clients as she researched, not to add information to the books, but to create an authenticity that came from slipping into her client's memories as best she could. She also reviewed previous notes and research material, making new connections since she was more familiar with the people involved.

As often happened, all the stress and worry of the day slipped out of her head as she found her groove, the mental spot where her whole focus was on the job. One of the best things about being a writer was how all-consuming it could be when she gave herself over to it. It was a respite from all the other worries of life.

When she noticed the time at the bottom of her computer screen, she realized the afternoon had flashed by in what felt like a few minutes. She would have to stop and freshen up if she hoped to be downstairs in time for dinner, and she did not intend to be late.

When she finally slipped out into the hall, she remembered Thomas saying he didn't want his grandmother wandering around alone, so instead of heading for the stairs right away, she started in search of

Mariette's room. Her boss had said she had a suite nearby, so logically it must have been one of the others along the same corridor. Poppy rapped on each door and called out Mariette's name, but received no answer. Finally she had to give up, having run out of doors. Mariette had probably gone downstairs while Poppy was working. She'd been deep in the zone and wouldn't have heard footsteps coming down the hall.

With a shrug, she picked up her pace as she strode to the stairs, moving along at a good clip since the time she'd spent searching for Mariette meant she'd likely be last to the table. She was right. Mariette welcomed her as she stepped into the room, and Poppy felt heat creep into her face.

"Sorry," Poppy said as she hurried to the empty chair beside Thomas. "I was making notes and got caught up in the work."

"No need to apologize," Mariette said. "I heartily approve of a strong work ethic."

With Poppy finally seated and surrounded by moody faces, the dinner was served. No one was even trying to be cheerful. Though she could still hear the wind howling outside and she couldn't help but worry about the broken boat, Poppy made an effort to savor the meal, if only because she was grateful for the people who'd experienced the same stress as everyone else but still managed to create amazing food.

Cook had made a traditional New England boiled dinner, but the quality of the cooking elevated the simple fare. The corned beef was tender and perfectly seasoned. The cabbage and potatoes were rich and buttery. Spiced carrots completed the meal.

While she ate, Poppy noticed that Arthur escorted Mrs. Bing to and from the kitchen with the food. "You're not alone in thinking we shouldn't wander the house by ourselves," she said to Thomas.

He started, as if her comment had cut into deep thoughts. "Actually, I believe Mrs. Bing has been upset all afternoon."

"Has something happened?" Poppy asked.

"You mean other than Jackie's death and the bashed-in boat?" Teddy asked.

"And don't forget finding you 'dead,'" Cecil said, grinning at Teddy.

Teddy snorted. "The reports of my death were greatly exaggerated."

Cecil raised both eyebrows. "Teddy Marcone, I am shocked. That was almost a literary allusion."

Teddy narrowed his eyes. "I don't know what that means, but if you're making fun of me, don't bother." He shoved a forkful of corned beef in his mouth and chewed without further comment.

"So nothing else has happened?" Poppy asked quickly, hoping to sidetrack the men.

"Nothing at all," Mariette said. "Some people are easily rattled."

"It isn't that easy," Mrs. Bing said, who had just returned through the servant's door with Arthur. "I assume you're talking about me. I happen to know that housekeepers are always the expendable ones in scary movies. No one even knows their names before they end up dead."

"This is not a movie, dear," Mariette said.

"Fine, but just so you all know, my name is Betty," Mrs. Bing said. "So if I'm murdered in my sleep, please, don't call me 'the housekeeper.' I'd want people to remember me by name."

Teddy snorted again. "Your name is Betty Bing?" He burst into loud, braying laughter.

The housekeeper drew herself up sharply to face him, anger evident in her features, which simply made Teddy laugh harder. Poppy felt terrible for the poor woman. It must have been difficult enough to be so afraid without having someone laugh at her.

When Teddy finally laughed himself out, the housekeeper said, "My name is Elizabeth Ann Wilson Bing. My friends call me Betty."

Her nose wrinkled as her gaze swept the room, making it clear that no one present would ever fit the description.

"I think your concerns are completely sensible," Thomas said. "I don't believe anyone should wander around alone until the police arrive. And I recommend everyone lock their doors at night."

"That's fine for all of you," Mrs. Bing said in a tone that caused Arthur to lay a hand on her arm, possibly hoping to remind her that she was all but shouting at her boss's grandson. Mrs. Bing shook it off. "Cook and I will be all alone in the lighthouse keeper's cottage. We're practically begging to be murdered when we walk home at night."

"I expect you'll be fine," Mariette said. "But I do agree that neither of you should have to go outside in this weather. You can stay in the house. I'm certain we have the room." Her attention shifted to Arthur. "Can you take care of that?"

"Of course."

Mrs. Bing blinked rapidly in apparent surprise at the offer. "That's kind of you, ma'am. Thank you. And I'm sure Cook would thank you too. We'll rest easier being in here."

Teddy raised an eyebrow. "You do realize that if there *is* a killer, you'll be in here with him or her now." At the last word, he stared at Mariette in clear accusation.

Mariette grinned in reply.

Mrs. Bing picked up her pitcher again, refilled water glasses, and scurried out to get the dessert. Arthur followed her. Poppy waited to see if any fresh conversation would spring up, but everyone was staring thoughtfully into their dinners, so she directed her attention to hers as well.

When the last of the food was gone, Mariette stood as Mrs. Bing and Arthur cleared plates. "Let us all retire to the dining room. Arthur, please stay with Mrs. Bing and Cook while they clear up after dinner and accompany them as they settle into rooms. No one is to move about the house alone."

"I refuse to travel in a pack like a frightened dog," Cecil said fiercely.

"Me neither," Teddy chimed in. "I can take care of myself."

"Hush, both of you," Mariette said. "I'll speak with you two in the drawing room."

Thomas stifled a groan at the dark expressions the two men directed toward his grandmother. He wished desperately that his grandmother wasn't so dedicated to purposely agitating dangerous men. Since Cecil and Teddy made up Thomas's entire suspect list for the possible murder of Jacqueline, Mariette's constant goading of both worried him.

Cecil and Teddy left, with Teddy stomping out his displeasure and Cecil radiating his in a more controlled blast of cool fury. The men were quite different, but Thomas could see either one of them being pushed to murder. He stepped over and slid his arm into his grandmother's arm. "Could you please stop trying to get yourself killed?"

"I don't know what you're talking about," Mariette argued imperiously.

"I'm talking about intentionally riling up Cecil and Teddy."

"I am not afraid of those knuckleheads."

"Splendid," Thomas said. "But they worry me, and so does your reckless behavior."

She beamed up at him. "You always were a worrywart. I remember when you were a child, you'd race through the house and tell us about safety hazards. I said you'd make a great safety inspector someday."

Thomas heard a light giggle behind them and knew Mariette had managed to amuse Poppy. "Too bad I missed my calling," he said dryly as they walked out of the dining room and into the hall.

"It really is," Mariette said. "You stay too closed up in stuffy colleges. You're becoming a dreadful nag. I wonder if you shouldn't try some interesting hobby. Maybe racing cars or leaping out of airplanes."

"Are you trying to get rid of me?" Thomas asked as he peered down at his grandmother's teasing face.

She patted his cheek. "Never."

The beautiful mahogany double doors of the drawing room were open. Cecil and Teddy stood close to the fireplace where a fire already burned. "When did Arthur have time to set a fire?" Thomas asked.

"Before dinner," Mariette answered. "After Poppy and I finished working, I spent some time in here, and Arthur made up a fire for me."

"Alone?" Thomas said, careful to keep his voice calm.

"Of course he did it alone. The man has years of experience."

"No, Mariette, I was asking if you sat in this room alone for hours when someone could easily hurt you."

"I chatted with Arthur for a while," Mariette said easily, "but mostly, yes. If you were worried about me, you could have come down and found me."

Thomas was annoyed with himself for not realizing his grandmother was taking foolish risks. He'd spent his afternoon hoofing it down to the boat again to examine the hole and check the area for whatever tool might have been used to make it. He hadn't been able to find one, though he had noticed that the storm was lessening. When he'd finally done all he could, Thomas had shivered all the way back to the house and stood in the shower for at least fifteen minutes until his teeth stopped chattering. For at least part of that time, his grandmother had been a sitting duck without his knowledge.

"Why don't we all have a nice civilized glass of brandy to calm our nerves?" Mariette suggested to the room at large.

"I'll pass," Thomas said. "It isn't in anyone's best interest to cloud their judgment right now."

Mariette laughed. "You have entirely too much faith in the strength of my brandy on a full stomach. But suit yourself." She began pouring brandy into snifters.

"None for me," Teddy said, holding up a glass. "I already poured myself a whiskey. I'll leave the brandy for the posh among our group."

Poppy accepted a snifter from Mariette, but Thomas noticed that she swirled the glass absently without sipping from it. She studied each person, and Thomas suspected the attentive young woman didn't miss much.

"I never thought of brandy being particularly posh," Thomas said to Teddy. He hoped to redirect as much attention and potential ire from his grandmother as possible.

"That's because you're posh to the bone, boy," Teddy said. "Born with a silver spoon halfway down your throat."

"That sounds uncomfortable," Poppy observed with a grin.

"Doesn't it?" Thomas said.

"I had to work for what I have," Teddy insisted. "No one ever gave me anything."

"Don't be tiresome, Teddy," Cecil said wearily. "Joseph and I gave you plenty. We practically dragged you out of trouble several times."

"And I should be grateful? Is that what you're saying?"

"Maybe less whiny at least," Cecil said. "You haven't suffered as much as you like to claim."

Teddy gulped down the last of the whiskey in his glass and slammed it down on the table. He moved closer to Cecil, invading the other man's space. "You need to show more respect."

"As soon as it's deserved," Cecil said.

Thomas studied the two men, not sure what to do. He wouldn't mind listening to Teddy bluster, as something honest and unexpected might come from it, but he wasn't interested in another fistfight. With Teddy and Cecil, there was always an edge to their bickering, always a sense of short fuses on the verge of sparking.

"I deserve respect!" Teddy roared. "I have taken enough of your superior attitude, Cecil. I'm not the idiot you make me out to be. I always saw and knew what was going on, even the things you thought you'd hidden so well."

"Teddy, you need to calm down," Cecil said, his voice low.

Thomas doubted Cecil had Teddy's best interests at heart, but Thomas agreed with the statement. As Teddy railed and jabbed his finger at Cecil over and over, his face was growing redder and reader.

"Maybe we should all take a step away from this conflict," Thomas suggested.

Teddy spun on him and bellowed, "Shut up!" Then his mouth snapped closed and his eyes bulged. He clutched at his chest, the fabric of his collared shirt bunching under thick fingers. His mouth opened and closed several times.

"Teddy?" Mariette said. "You should sit down."

"She's right," Cecil said. He reached out and caught Teddy's arm. "Let's have a seat."

Teddy didn't resist. Instead, his knees simply buckled, and he was too heavy for Cecil to hold up on his own. Thomas leaped to catch Teddy's other arm, but he wasn't quick enough and the man ended up on the floor.

"It must be that blood pressure thing again," Mariette said. "We should elevate his feet." She directed the next remark at Poppy. "Isn't that right?"

"Yes ma'am." Poppy knelt beside Teddy, and Thomas joined her. She pressed her fingers against Teddy's neck. "No pulse, and I don't think he's breathing."

Thomas began CPR immediately, grateful that he'd learned it years before when he'd first become a professor. It was all part of his desire never to be caught unprepared. But though he kept the CPR going for a long time as Poppy joined in with breaths into Teddy's gaping mouth, they couldn't save him.

Teddy Marcone was dead.

Finally Thomas stopped the compressions and sat up, his arms aching, and looked at his grandmother. "I'm sorry."

Mariette's hand was pressed to her chest, and her eyes were damp. "Poor Teddy. I had no idea his health was so bad."

"You know, Mariette, your friend group is declining at an alarming rate."

"Thank you, Cecil," Mariette snapped. "I've noticed."

Poppy rose to her feet. "Considering what he said earlier about refusing to wear compression socks, I'm not sure he took good care of himself. He may have had heart problems."

"Perhaps," Mariette agreed.

Thomas couldn't see how Teddy's death could have occurred due to anything other than natural causes. No one had touched the man, and they'd all eaten the same food.

Although, Thomas thought, *Teddy was alone in drinking the whiskey.* As the others argued, Thomas quietly picked up Teddy's whiskey glass.

He wanted the glass reserved for police testing if they discovered Teddy's death wasn't as natural as they assumed.

9

$\mathcal{A}$s they gazed bleakly down at Teddy, Thomas surveyed the group standing in a loose circle around a man who had so recently been hale and blustering. Poppy was frozen in place, stunned. Mariette was sad, and Cecil was unreadable.

Mariette finally tore her attention away from the still figure. "Obviously, Teddy cannot wait in here until the police arrive. I imagine the best choice is to put him in the conservatory. As we've noted previously, it's viciously cold out there."

"That would be the best plan. I'll need some help moving him though." Thomas supposed he could drag the poor man, but that felt disrespectful. Picking him up was out of the question. "Teddy was no lightweight."

"I will pass on this duty," Cecil said. "My goal is to survive this weekend, and hauling Teddy around would not be conducive to that."

"Arthur will help," Mariette said. "Poppy, be a dear and go get him. I imagine he's in the kitchen guarding the others."

"Wait," Thomas said. "Poppy shouldn't be alone."

Mariette peered at him, but he couldn't guess what was going on behind her cool expression. "Then go with her," she said finally.

Thomas was torn. He couldn't leave Mariette alone with Cecil. After Teddy's death, Cecil had moved up to his number one suspect. And since Cecil was the best suspect, he supposed Poppy was safer away from him. But he hated the thought of her being on her own, in case he was wrong about Cecil. The frustration made him growl under his breath.

"I'll be fine," Poppy assured him. "The kitchen isn't far, and I'm fairly good at taking care of myself."

"Good girl," Mariette said.

Thomas wished Poppy were not quite so confident, but he watched her dash from the room without further comment, despite the sick feeling that it was a mistake to let her go off on her own.

The empty hallways were something of a relief after the tension in the drawing room. Poppy made her way through the slightly dim hall to the front stairs and from there to the dining room. She didn't know if there was a more direct route to the kitchen, but she figured it would be easier for her to find it through the half-hidden servant's door in the corner of the dining room.

In the dining room, someone had shut off the lights, reducing the long table and chairs to shadowy shapes. The curtains hadn't been drawn over the windows, and the snow beat against the glass. Snow had stuck to the corners of the windows, making the viewing area smaller. Poppy wondered if it was possible for the blizzard to rage for so long that it completely obscured the windows with ice and snow. The thought of not being able to see outside at all made her shudder.

She carefully skirted the dining room table, heading for a door that was nearly invisible in the dark. She opened the door and found the hall even darker, but as she closed the servant's door behind her, she heard a slight clatter in the distance. She walked as quickly as she dared through the hall and was glad to see a light ahead. She reached the kitchen doors, which were hung to swing easily when pushed. Light seeped all the way around the door.

Poppy pushed through the door and into the kitchen. She was impressed by the starkly modern room with abundant cupboards and bright stainless-steel appliances. Mrs. Bing was kneeling in front of the open oven door, scrubbing something inside, while Cook stood at the sink, washing a large pot. In the far corner, near what Poppy guessed was the staff dining table, the butler leaned against the wall and sipped coffee.

As soon as Poppy stepped through the doorway, Cook lifted the pot out of the soapy water and offered a bright smile. "Can we help you, Miss?"

"Arthur?" Poppy said. "You're needed in the drawing room."

"I am?" Arthur said in surprise. "Does Mrs. Winter want coffee for her guests?"

"I don't think so," Poppy said. "There's a problem. Mr. Marcone collapsed, and we weren't able to help him. I'm afraid he's dead."

Cook dropped the pot back into the sink. Poppy caught her fearful expression, though the woman didn't say anything.

"Was it the same thing that made him fall before?" Mrs. Bing asked as she rose to her feet, a ball of steel wool held loosely in one hand.

"We don't know," Poppy said. "We tried CPR for a long time, but it didn't help. I think he may have had heart problems."

"That's terrible," Mrs. Bing said. "Everything about this weekend is terrible. It's enough to make me wonder about the story of the curse."

"Simpleminded drivel," Arthur retorted before taking a more polite tone with Poppy. "What specifically does Mrs. Winter want me to do?"

"You'll need to bring the key for the conservatory," Poppy said. "And Thomas needs help moving Teddy in there."

"I thought Arthur was going to stay with us," Mrs. Bing said. "And he was going to help us find rooms after we finished the chores here."

"I will," Arthur said. "I cannot imagine it will take long to help Mr. Nordwich."

"Didn't Mrs. Winter say you shouldn't leave us alone?" Mrs. Bing asked.

"And now she wants me in the drawing room. The situation has changed. I would have thought dealing with changing situations was something you were told to expect when you took this job."

"Dead people weren't mentioned in the interview," Mrs. Bing said tartly. Poppy saw Arthur frown, but Poppy thought the housekeeper's display of spirit was a good sign. If Mrs. Bing were annoyed with Arthur, she'd forget to be afraid.

"You may come with me if you wish," Arthur said, though Poppy could tell by his voice that he wouldn't wish it.

"And see a dead body?" Mrs. Bing said. "No thank you. Besides I don't want to leave Cook alone."

"You and Cook will be fine," Arthur set his coffee cup down on the counter.

"And if the murderer comes in and kills us both?" the housekeeper demanded.

Arthur spoke with an almost theatrical level of patience. "We do not know that there has been a murder. Thus we do not know that there is a murderer."

"I can stay with you both," Poppy offered, wanting to get Arthur going. She suspected Thomas would worry if too much time passed before Arthur showed up in the drawing room. "I've taken some extensive self-defense classes, since I travel so much. I believe we should be perfectly fine between the three of us."

"That sounds good," Cook said, speaking before Mrs. Bing could lodge a complaint. "We've got lots of potential weapons in here too. I can't imagine anyone would want to mess with us."

"I suppose you're right," Mrs. Bing conceded.

"Then it's decided," Arthur said briskly. "You will all stay here while I am gone. I shouldn't be long." He reached into his pocket and pulled out a key. "And I have been carrying the key to the conservatory, so that will not be a problem." With that, he strode out of the room without a backward glance.

Poppy offered the two women her friendliest smile. "Can I help with the cleanup? I don't mind washing dishes. I've done my fair share of it."

Mrs. Bing gaped at her. "Certainly not. Guests do not work in the kitchen. I'm certain it would be as good as my job if I were to let that happen."

"I'm not a guest," Poppy said. "I work for Mrs. Winter, the same as you."

"I don't think it's quite the same," Cook said. "But it's nice of you to want to help. We're actually nearly done. I could make us some tea or coffee if you want."

"Coffee wouldn't be a good idea," Mrs. Bing said. "I doubt I'll sleep a wink as it is."

"How about some lovely butterfly pea flower tea? It's healthy, caffeine-free, and delicious," Cook said as she bustled over to the electric kettle.

Poppy considered reminding her that there was still a pot in the sink but decided against it. Instead she said, "Tea would be nice. You have a great kitchen to work in. From the outside appearance, you almost expect woodburning stoves and gaslights."

Cook chuckled. "I know. I thought that myself when I got here, then I saw this. It's the nicest kitchen I've ever been in. And Mrs. Winter spares no expense on the ingredients either, so I don't have to make do with wilted produce or food from cans. It's an absolute pleasure to cook here." She winced. "Except for the murders."

"I doubt Teddy was murdered, since he had some kind of chronic condition," Poppy said.

"It's still terrible," Mrs. Bing cut in.

"That's true," Poppy agreed.

"So," Cook said as she collected three clear glass mugs from a cupboard. "You're a writer?"

"A ghostwriter."

Cook grinned as she poured water into the mugs. "You strike me as lively enough."

Poppy laughed. "That is a morbid name for it, isn't it? It means that I write books for other people. This time I'm writing Mrs. Winter's memoir."

Cook added a tea bag to each mug, watching the water turn a vivid blue. "If half the rumors I've heard are true, that'll be a juicy one."

"We shouldn't be talking about that," Mrs. Bing said primly.

"Of course." Cook handed out the mugs, then collected a sugar bowl from another cupboard and a small bowl of lemon wedges from the fridge. "If you add lemon to the tea, it shifts from blue to purple, like magic."

Poppy tried the cook's suggestion and admired the lovely color change. She took a sip. "That is good."

Cook winked. "Told you."

Poppy nodded toward the other side of the room, where two doors led out of the kitchen opposite where she'd come in. "Where do those go?"

"The left one goes out to a mudroom," Mrs. Bing explained. "And then you can get outside from there. I think there's a small chef's garden."

"Not that anything is growing this time of year," Cook said. "Nothing grows in a blizzard."

"And the other door?"

Cook and Mrs. Bing exchanged a glance, which piqued Poppy's interest. "It's a short hallway," Cook said hesitantly.

"To where?" Poppy pressed.

"The lighthouse," Cook said.

"How exciting. What's the lighthouse like?"

"I have no idea." Cook's voice made it clear that was a huge disappointment.

"It's off-limits," Mrs. Bing explained. "Arthur's rule. And I have no interest in seeing it anyway. If there's any place in this house that is going to be haunted, that would be it."

"I hadn't thought of that." Cook put her hands on her hips. "Perhaps it's better that we can't go up."

Poppy found the idea of an off-limits tower to be irresistible. And Mariette had told her that she was free to roam around the house. "I believe I will go and see it." She set her mug on the counter and headed across the room.

"You said you'd stay with us," Mrs. Bing reminded her.

"You're welcome to come with me," Poppy said.

"Arthur would be furious with us," Cook said, but she didn't sound particularly cowed by the thought. "I'm in."

"I can't stay here alone," Mrs. Bing protested.

"I'm sure you'll be fine," Poppy said. "But you may be happier with us."

Mrs. Bing groaned. "Fine, I'll come. But I'm telling Arthur you made me."

"You can tell him anything you wish," Poppy said. She wasn't sure how well she'd be able to placate the butler, but she was fairly certain Mariette would take their part. Her boss admired strong-willed women.

Poppy led the way into the hall. As with everywhere else she went in the house, the hall was scrupulously clean, so though it could have been brighter, it wasn't particularly ominous. And there were no ghosts.

She walked along to an arched opening that led to an old part of the house with stone floors and walls, and steep stairs. No effort had been made to modernize there. She groped along the wall for a switch and flipped it on. Bare light bulbs set in fixtures close to the wall cast an anemic glow.

Poppy peered up the stairs as far as she could see. The steps themselves were well-worn but in good shape. She could tell the walls weren't offering the insulation of the rest of the house. It was distinctly chilly.

"Here we go," Poppy said, trying for a cheery sound, but finding she barely whispered instead. Annoyed by her own reaction, she immediately started up the stairs. She'd barely climbed half a dozen steps before she heard Cook speak up. She was still near the bottom, behind Mrs. Bing.

"I enjoy an adventure now and then, but this is too scary," Cook said. "I'm going to wait in the kitchen after all. I guess I'll finish washing that pot."

"By yourself?" Mrs. Bing asked.

"I'm not afraid of the kitchen," Cook said. She clomped down the few steps and vanished into the hall.

The housekeeper squinted up past Poppy, then gave her an apologetic shrug. "I'm going to go and watch over Cook. I'd be in so much trouble if someone killed her while I was up here violating one of Arthur's rules."

"You'd best go then," Poppy agreed, though the reminder that Arthur didn't want anyone in the tower simply made her want to see it all the more. After all, it was an important part of the history of Winterhouse. She had to see it to fully understand and therefore accurately represent it in Mariette's memoir.

"Good luck," Mrs. Bing said. She was already hurrying down the steps.

Poppy watched the woman until she disappeared, then resumed climbing the stone steps. As she went, she could hear the storm outside, though the moaning of the wind was muffled by the stone walls. Poppy was surprised the blizzard hadn't blown itself out yet. Even in New England, it was a lot of wind for a long time.

"Realistically, it should be done by morning," she told herself. She'd hoped the sound of her own voice would be comforting, but somehow it sounded intrusive in the tower. *You're getting jumpy.* She'd be glad to see the police tomorrow, assuming the storm was done. It was high time they had outside help.

As she continued up the cold steps, Poppy wondered how far she'd be able to see from the top of the lighthouse. In the storm, visibility would be less, but she considered it probable she'd see the lights of the village. As she walked, she noticed strange echoes in the tower. It was almost as if someone else were climbing the stairs, though she seriously doubted either Cook or the housekeeper had changed their minds and decided to join her, especially considering the cold and the lack of decent light on the steps.

Now that she thought about it, shouldn't there be more light? The steep steps were potentially dangerous. Of course, she assumed Mariette never came up here. And updating the lighthouse would be expensive, especially if it was never used.

That's when Poppy realized she heard sounds from above, not below. That didn't make sense at all, since Poppy was confident no one else was in the tower. She'd seen everyone in the household within the last thirty minutes. There would have been no time to get up into the tower. *It's some kind of weird sound illusion.* She picked up her pace so she could reach the top and solve the mystery of the impossible noises.

Surely she was almost there, though it was hard to tell with the winding stairs and lack of windows.

Then she came around one of the tight curves to find herself facing a female figure on the stairs. The ghost story had affected Poppy more than she'd expected, because the sight of the woman dressed in white threw her into a panic. She yelped and jumped back instinctively, forgetting she was on the stairs. There was nothing but air under her feet.

She pinwheeled her arms frantically, knowing there was no chance she'd be able to catch herself. A fall down the steep stone stairs was going to be bad. Really bad.

10

Though her life didn't quite flash before her eyes, Poppy was still shocked when she didn't tumble to her death. Instead the strange figure rushed at her and a hand grabbed the front of Poppy's thick sweater. The figure braced herself on the stone wall and jerked Poppy to her feet. The pulling didn't stop there. The stranger hauled Poppy close and demanded, "Who are you?"

Poppy didn't immediately answer. She was struggling to catch her breath from the rush of adrenaline. She could barely believe she hadn't tumbled down the stone steps.

"Who am I?" Poppy echoed finally, the woman's words slow to penetrate her stunned surprise. "Who are *you*? I'm pretty sure you're not supposed to be here."

"I'm Bethany Nordwich," the woman replied. "This is my family's home. I can be here any time I choose. Now, tell me who you are."

Poppy took a deep breath, searching for the tattered remains of her calm, professional attitude. "I work for your mother. I'm Poppy Hayes. Your mother doesn't know you're here, does she? How did you get here, anyway?"

The woman groaned. "Of course you work for Mother." She turned away from Poppy and continued up the stairs. "You may as well come too. It's too cold to talk on the stairs."

Curiosity drove Poppy after her. She was beginning to wonder if she'd chased a white rabbit into a weekend where absolutely nothing made sense. When they reached the top of the lighthouse, it was clear that while the tower stairs had not been updated at all, the room at the top definitely had. The original lighthouse lamp was gone, and the room had been transformed into a round sitting room with a beautiful wrought iron daybed, presently made up with a pile of quilts. The room also held several comfortable chairs, and an electric heater that had done a decent job of bringing the temperature up. Built-in bookshelves lined the walls all around the room. Most of the remaining floor space was taken up with a small table and two chairs. On the table, Poppy spotted an electric kettle, and nearby was a tiny fridge.

"Would you care for some tea?" Bethany asked. "It's not freezing up here, but it's not exactly balmy either. I find that frequent doses of hot tea help."

"That would be nice," Poppy said, examining her unexpected hostess. Like Mariette, Bethany was a handsome woman, tall and slender. She had shoulder-length auburn hair gathered into a loose ponytail and wore a thick white cotton sweater, white fleece pants, and sneakers. Despite the casual clothes, there was an air of elegance about the woman.

Poppy settled into a chair at the table while Bethany made tea. She found she was eager for the hot drink. She'd never gotten more than a sip or two of the mug of tea Cook had made for her, and she could use something warm after the cold climb. "I'm surprised the heater can make it so warm in a room with all these windows."

"The windows have all been replaced," Bethany said as she busied herself with the kettle and floral china cups. "These were pricey custom pieces that are amazingly well-insulated. My parents had this renovated because I loved spending hours up here with a book and my mother worried that I'd catch pneumonia someday. It was a surprise for my thirteenth birthday."

"It's beautiful." Poppy would have loved the room when she was a teenager, but her hard-working parents couldn't give her fancy tower rooms, even if they'd wanted to.

"It is," Bethany agreed. "I always felt safe here. I think it was a result of being surrounded by proof of how much my parents once loved me."

Poppy considered taking the bait, but she had bigger questions. "How did you get onto the island without anyone knowing?"

"Obviously, I couldn't." She took a tiny pitcher from the fridge. "I prefer milk in my tea. I have sugar too, but no lemon. I never put lemon in tea. Will you be okay without it?"

"I'll be fine," Poppy said. "So how did you get to the island?"

"I rented a boat. I'm quite experienced with boats, having grown up on an island. And I know the waters around this island better than anyone alive. I tied up in a tiny natural cove where I used to swim sometimes when I lived here. It's relatively sheltered, so I have high hopes that the boat will still be there after the blizzard passes."

"And who knows you're here?" Poppy asked. Surely Mariette wasn't simply pretending to be upset that her daughter hadn't come.

"Arthur. He let me in after I walked up from the cove. He's been bringing me food. No one else knows I'm here."

Poppy understood Arthur's rule about not going up to the lighthouse tower. "He must know Mariette won't approve of that kind of secret."

"Arthur has known me since I was a baby. He's my family, or as good as. Plus, I don't think he's afraid of my mother."

"Why not tell her that you're here?"

"I will," Bethany said as she began pouring hot water over tea bags in the china cups. "I intended to speak to her at once, but then I found out about Teddy, Cecil, Matthew, and Jacqueline coming for the weekend. I always liked Matthew, who was funny and kind. But I despise the others, and I'm fairly certain the feeling is mutual.

I intended to stay out of sight until they left, and then I'd talk to my mother about this outrageous memoir."

Bethany placed one of the two teacups in front of Poppy, then sank into the other seat. "The view from up here is amazing when there's no storm."

"I can imagine," Poppy said. She hoped to have a chance to see it sometime. But first they had to get through the storm. She watched Bethany sip her tea. The woman seemed perfectly composed, and Poppy began to suspect she had no idea what was going on. "Has Author told you about what's happening?"

"He told me everyone is stuck here because of the storm," Bethany said. "And I know Matthew didn't come. I don't blame him. I doubt he is any fonder of those loathsome people than I am. But Arthur hasn't had time to sit and talk. I'm sure there's been drama. There's always drama with that group."

Poppy sipped her tea and considered how to ease into the topic of the deaths. As she did, she watched her hostess, who was studying her in kind. Bethany had Mariette's eyes, though the rest of her facial structure was quite different, probably inherited from her father.

From her knowledge of Mariette's age and Thomas's, Poppy guessed the woman was in her early sixties, and the laugh lines at the corners of her eyes suggested Poppy was right. Then Poppy told herself to stop stalling. Cataloging the woman's features wasn't going to make telling her the truth any easier.

"I'm sorry to be the one to tell you," Poppy said. "But Matthew didn't come because he was murdered. And last night Jacqueline died here in the conservatory."

Bethany's expression sharpened. "Died here? How?"

"It may have been an accident," Poppy said. "Her skull was damaged. I found her in the conservatory this morning."

Bethany's hand rose slowly to her mouth, and her gaze dropped to the calm surface of her tea. "How horrible. I detested her, really. I thought she was one of the most awful women I'd ever met. But still. Mother must be terribly upset."

"She's handling it well," Poppy said, mostly because she wasn't sure what Mariette was feeling. The older woman kept her emotions hidden much of the time. "Teddy is dead too. He died in the last hour or so. I think it was probably some kind of heart attack. Apparently he had medical problems"

"Wow. Where was that?"

"In the drawing room," Poppy explained. "After dinner."

Bethany rocked back in her chair. "I don't know what to think or feel. Teddy always struck me as a thug, and I couldn't imagine why my father was involved with him. Jacqueline was catty and said ugly things to me more than once when I was a child, though never in front of my parents." She shook her head. "But still, dead. I guess I thought they were the same as my mother—indestructible."

"No one is indestructible," Poppy said.

Bethany picked up a spoon and stirred her tea, though she hadn't added anything to it. Poppy suspected it was a soothing gesture. "The people in the village," she murmured. "They think this island is cursed. Growing up, I loved it here, but now, hearing this . . . Maybe I'm the one who has been wrong."

"The ferry boat captain told me about that curse," Poppy said.

Bethany smirked. "Cass loves that story. He has always loved any tale that is critical of my family, even when we were kids. You'd hardly know it now, but we were friends of a sort at one time. He always reminded me of one of the lost boys in Peter Pan—wild and perhaps too easily led." She took the spoon from the cup and set it precisely down on the table. "How do things change so much?"

Since Poppy had no answer for that, she stuck to the topic of the deaths. "Can you think of anyone who would want Matthew or Jacqueline hurt?"

Bethany shrugged. "I couldn't say. My parents kept me in the dark about a lot of their life. Mother now insists my father did some bad things, but I don't know whether I believe her. He was a wonderful father. How could he be a terrible person?"

Poppy didn't have an answer to that either, though she knew people were often a complicated mix of good and bad.

Bethany stood again. "I think I have some cookies to go with the tea."

"I'm fine," Poppy said. She took a sip of the hot tea, wrapping her fingers around the cup and enjoying the warmth. "This is excellent."

"It's imported. Nothing but the best for Winterhouse." Bethany's tone didn't make the words sound complimentary. Suddenly, she towered over Poppy, which gave her next words an almost ominous edge. "I would rather no one else knew I was here."

Poppy rose, preferring not to be loomed over. "I can't lie to your mother. She's my boss."

"It wouldn't have to be a lie. I doubt Mother is going to ask you if you happened across someone in the lighthouse."

"That's still dishonest," Poppy said.

Bethany walked over to the nearest window and spoke without facing Poppy. "Think about it, at least. If someone is hurting people here, it may be safer for me if no one knows I'm here."

"Or you may be in greater danger because you're isolated up here." Poppy placed her cup back on the table. "I'll have to tell them something. I've been gone from the drawing room for quite some time, and there will be questions. Besides, Cook and Mrs. Bing know I came up here."

"Arthur can keep them quiet," Bethany said. "And you're a writer.

Surely you can come up with something believable that doesn't include me."

"The easiest answer is for you to simply come downstairs with me and let your mother know you're here."

Bethany gave her an almost pitying smile. "That would not be simple."

Frustrated, Poppy was trying to come up with another way to convince Bethany to come downstairs when she heard someone shouting her name on the other side of the door to the stairs. She recognized that voice immediately. It was Thomas, and that meant Bethany's secret was about to come out, whether she wanted it to or not.

Thomas was chilled and slightly winded as he charged into the tower room. Poppy's name was on his lips, but he stood silent and frozen at the sight of his mother, standing calmly near one of the lighthouse windows with a china cup in her hands.

"Mother, what are you doing here?" he stammered.

His mother glared at him, resembling Mariette more than ever. "This is still my home. One of them anyway."

"She rented a boat and brought herself," Poppy told him, drawing his attention to her. He would be sure to have a word with her about disappearing and worrying everyone half to death, but that could wait.

Poppy continued, "The butler has been keeping her secret and caring for her."

"But why are you hiding?" Thomas asked Bethany.

"To avoid Mother's guests," Bethany said. "I never could stand those people and wasn't going to be polite over meals with them. I may have had to keep my distaste for them to myself when I was a child, but I'm not a child anymore."

"And you think Mariette would have insisted you be polite?" Thomas asked.

"Of course she would have. But Poppy tells me that is an ever-shrinking problem."

"That kind of talk would upset Mariette." He crossed his arms over his chest. "None of what you've said answers my core question. Why have you come here now? I've been trying to get you and Mariette to reconcile since we learned of her diagnosis. You said you wouldn't step foot on the island until she died."

His mother mirrored his stance. "I changed my mind."

"But why?"

"To talk to Mother. Thomas, you have to know she can't write this memoir. She'll ruin our lives even more than she already has. I thought I'd stay up here until those horrible people left, then I would talk some sense into Mother. You've been telling me she wanted to reconcile. Well, parading our lives in front of the world is not the way to do that. I can't believe you haven't talked her out of it by now."

"You honestly believe Mariette would listen to me?" Thomas asked, fighting a frustrated urge to shout. He loved his mother and grandmother. But sometimes dealing with the two of them made him want to run away to Europe and hide out.

"This may not be the time for an argument," Poppy said. "But I can't believe it's safe for your mother to be up here all alone. Something is going on in this house, and having people off on their own isn't going to help us solve anything."

"A good point," Thomas said. "One you should have thought of before you left the kitchen to come up here alone."

Poppy's face darkened, but he couldn't tell if she was angry or embarrassed, and she didn't say anything to make it clear.

Bethany stepped between Thomas and Poppy and glared at him, hands on her hips. "And what makes you think you can tell me or anyone else what to do?"

"Really?" Thomas asked. "Are you honestly going to play the 'you're not the boss of me' card? Mom, people are dying. You have to come downstairs. Otherwise, we'll need to bring everyone up here, because we all need to stay together. It's the best chance we have of staying safe. And if your reason for being up here is to avoid Mariette's guests, that's not a big problem. Cecil is the only one left."

"Saving the worst for last," Bethany said.

"That's it. I don't have time to argue with you." Thomas spun on his heels. "I'll go get everyone else and bring them up here even if I have to carry Mariette up the stairs."

"No," Bethany said. "I don't want Cecil up here contaminating my space. I'll come down, under protest."

The three of them trudged down the stairs. Thomas found his thoughts were a whirl. He'd been worried when Poppy didn't return with Arthur, but the pressing problem of Teddy's body kept him from going straight to the kitchen to collect her. After they had moved the body, he'd told Arthur to stay with Mariette, then gone straight to the kitchen. When he hadn't found Poppy there, he'd nearly panicked. He was growing fond of Poppy, but his worry for her had been out of proportion. Apparently the stresses of the weekend were wearing on him.

When they neared the bottom of the tower, Thomas heard Mariette's imperious voice. "Arthur, step aside. My grandson and one of my guests are up there, and I need to know they're okay."

"Calm down, Mariette." The voice was Cecil's. "We've had quite enough people having heart attacks or falling on their heads. You don't need to join them."

"Get out of my way," Mariette ordered.

Thomas was the first to emerge from the stairs and enter the hallway where the others stood. "You don't need to climb the stairs," he said. "We're here."

"About time," Mariette said. "Where's Poppy?"

"She's coming, but not alone."

Then Poppy emerged into the hallway, followed by Bethany.

All the color drained from Mariette's face, as if a ghost had come from the tower rather than her daughter.

"Wow, this is more of a welcoming committee than I expected," Bethany said, her tone cheery. Thomas suspected she was trying to break the shocked spell in the hallway.

"Bethany," Mariette said finally. The anger Thomas expected didn't arrive. Instead, Mariette ignited with joy. "You came after all. Though I have no idea exactly what's happening here."

Mariette stared at Arthur, who shifted under her gaze, distinctly uncomfortable. Behind him, Cook frowned with confusion and interest.

Cecil, on the other hand, was livid. "I guess we know who hit Jacqueline on the head now."

"What are you talking about?" Bethany said. "I haven't hit anyone on the head. I've been in the tower ever since I got here."

"So you say," Cecil retorted. "But you were a monster as a child, and now we know you were lurking in a secret part of the house, probably plotting our demise. We should lock you up until the police arrive."

"Stop talking foolishness," Mariette said. "My daughter didn't kill anyone. If she says she was in the tower all this time, that's what happened."

Judging from her open-mouthed stare, Bethany was shocked by her mother's support.

"You always were blind to the rotten brat," Cecil said. "If no one is going to do anything about this, I will." He took a step toward Bethany, but both Thomas and Arthur stepped into his path.

"Get out of my way," Cecil snarled.

"Not until you calm down," Thomas said, using the tone he reserved for students who tried to bully him into good grades they hadn't earned.

Cecil tried to stare Thomas down. He nearly had the strength of personality for the job, but the reality was that he wasn't a young man anymore. With an exasperated grunt, he stepped away. "Fine. But don't think I won't keep an eye on you," he said, speaking to Bethany over Thomas's shoulder. "I'm on to you, and you're not going to find me nearly as easy to kill."

"I don't want to kill you," Bethany said with false sweetness. "I simply want you to go away. Forever."

"That's enough, Bethany," Mariette said. "We're stuck here, so we're going to have to get along."

"Right." Bethany rolled her eyes, making Thomas wonder if there was something about being around a parent that transformed every adult into a teenager again.

"Excuse me," Poppy said. "Where is Mrs. Bing?"

Thomas scanned the group in the hallway. It was an excellent question.

"Isn't she up in the tower?" Cook asked. "She never came into the kitchen. I thought she went on up with you."

"No," Poppy said. "She said she was going to the kitchen to wait for Arthur with you. She said she didn't want to leave you alone."

"I never saw her," Cook said.

"Are we going to panic over a servant who wandered off?" Cecil asked. "I'm growing weary of rushing around the house in a panic whenever the hired help disappears."

"You're not worried?" Bethany said.

"Why should I be?" Cecil asked. "Unless you knocked Mrs. Bing on the head."

"I didn't knock anyone on the head," Bethany insisted.

"Stop talking," Mariette said. "Cecil, your behavior is growing increasingly beastly. Of course we're concerned about Mrs. Bing."

"Especially considering she wasn't really the type to wander off on her own," Poppy said. "Did she strike anyone else as particularly brave or particularly curious?"

"Not me," Cook said. "I thought she was going to climb into Arthur's pocket and hide when he left us in the kitchen." Then she raised her eyebrows. "Maybe she wanted to join the rest of you. She wouldn't have felt safe with only the two of us."

"In that case, we should probably check the kitchen first," Arthur said. "If she was searching for everyone and didn't find us, she may have gone to the kitchen after all."

"Good thinking," Mariette said.

The group filed into the kitchen, but the room was empty and silent other than the wind outside. Mrs. Bing wasn't there. But where could she be? And why would the fearful woman go wandering off on her own?

11

Thomas didn't argue when Mariette insisted they continue the search for Mrs. Bing. He also wanted to know where the housekeeper had gone.

"We shouldn't need to check the second floor," Arthur said. "I cannot imagine Mrs. Bing decided to go upstairs and tidy rooms."

"No," Thomas agreed. "That sounds improbable. Where do you think she is?"

Arthur shook his head. "I have no idea."

So they began the search. As they passed from room to room, Thomas found his attention drawn frequently to Poppy, whose intelligent eyes took in everything around her. Cook had a similar expression of curiosity and fascination, so the two women walked together. Thomas realized Cook probably hadn't seen much of the house beyond the kitchen, the dining area, and the lighthouse keeper's cottage. He was amazed that he'd never given that any thought before. Somewhere along the way, he'd begun to take servants for granted, and that bothered him. He didn't think of himself as the sort of man who stopped seeing people as people.

Poppy pulled him from his musings by calling over her shoulder, "Thomas, is this you?"

He caught up with her and examined the framed photo perched on the mantel in the drawing room. A boy with tousled hair stared solemnly out of the photo, clutching a well-worn stuffed bear. "Yes," he said.

"You were adorable," Poppy said.

"Good thing I outgrew it."

"We've seen everything downstairs," Cecil said sharply from the doorway. "Can we stop wasting time on a servant?"

"She's a scared young woman," Mariette retorted. "I don't expect you to feel anything for her, Cecil, but you could pretend to be a human being for a few minutes."

Cecil laughed. "So I shouldn't take my cue from you, then?"

Once again Thomas despaired of his grandmother's definition of friends, but he refused to be distracted. "As hard as it is to imagine," he said, "I'm beginning to wonder if Mrs. Bing went out to the lighthouse keeper's cottage. She may have remembered something she needed to move to her quarters here. Something she didn't want to talk about for some reason or other."

"She is tight-lipped about her stuff," Cook said. "She keeps her room locked at the cottage. I try not to take offense, but it's hard not to think she's worried about me stealing."

"Then we should go to the lighthouse keeper's cottage and see if she's there," Mariette said. "If she's not, we can check her rooms for a clue as to where she has gone. I've never known her to carry a cell phone."

"Not to argue with you, ma'am," Cook said. "But as I said, she locks her rooms. Unless you're going to force the doors."

"No need for that," Mariette said. "Arthur has master keys."

Thomas held up a hand to draw their attention to him. "I don't believe everyone needs to go to the lighthouse keeper's cottage. It's not a large building, and the weather is still punishing. I'll go out and search for Mrs. Bing. And everyone can wait here."

"You'll need Arthur and his keys," Mariette said.

"He can lend them to me," Thomas replied. "I want Arthur here to keep you all safe."

"I will protect them with my life," Arthur promised as he passed over a ring of keys.

"I do not need a protector," Bethany said.

"I am quite capable of taking care of myself," Mariette added. For a moment the two women wore nearly identical expressions of defiance. "You should take Arthur. I don't want you going out alone."

"Thomas won't be alone," Poppy said, her voice as firm as Mariette's or Bethany's. "I'll go with him. As I told Cook and Mrs. Bing, I've had extensive self-defense training, and I believe I can be helpful in a pinch."

"That will be acceptable," Mariette said. "Though I still think we should all go."

"You do not need to be out in the weather, Mariette," Thomas said sternly. "I don't think it subtracts any of your independence to recognize this weather is not a good combination with your illness, especially in light of the strain we've all been under."

"Fine. Go then. Arthur will keep the wolves at bay. And be careful. You're a college professor, not a superhero."

"I have no illusions about that," Thomas said. He left the room before the conversation could devolve any further, Poppy on his heels.

Once they were in the hall, heading for the door, Poppy said, "I thought you would argue about me coming along."

"Would that have done any good?" he asked.

"No, but it could have been fun." She beamed up at him, and he actually laughed, something he had not felt like doing for a while. He didn't mind having Poppy along, if only so he could keep an eye on her, considering that the last time she'd gone off on her own, she'd ended up in the lighthouse tower. He would have taken Mariette and his mother too if he weren't more worried about them being out in the weather than he was about them staying together in a group in the study.

Thomas shrugged into his heavy coat, then peered down at Poppy.

"You should be able to wear Mariette's coat." He took it from the rack. "I assume yours is upstairs."

"I also left my boots up there, but these shoes have a decent tread, so I should be fine." She took the coat from Thomas without argument and slipped into it.

Enjoying the chance to study her when she wasn't likely to notice as she buttoned the coat, Thomas pulled on his gloves without taking his eyes off her. He wished the circumstances weren't so dire. He had a dozen pointless questions he wanted to ask her, simply to hear her talk.

She fastened the last button and pulled a pair of mittens from one of the coat pockets. "What a nice surprise." With a grin, she held them up, then tilted her head. "What?"

"Excuse me?"

"You were staring at me funny," she said. "Do I look weird somehow? Cobwebs in my hair from the lighthouse tower? Crooked buttons? Tea leaves caught in my teeth?"

"None of the above. You're lovely. Put on the mittens. We need to get going." He hauled open the door, knowing that would put a quick stop to any further conversation. The cold flung itself at him, making his eyes sting, but he resisted the urge to slam the door and block out the wind. Instead, he and Poppy headed straight into the night, closing the door behind them.

Snow still fell thickly but as less of an angle. The wind whistled rather than howled, not that it felt any better when it threw icy snowflakes into their faces. "The storm has weakened considerably," Thomas said.

"It's almost pleasant," Poppy added, though her voice already held a shiver.

"The cottage is this way." Thomas stepped onto the snow-covered path. The snow wasn't deep, but he still wished he dared to take Poppy's hand, ostensibly to ensure she didn't slip on the slickened stone path.

He glanced over his shoulder and saw her picking her way carefully behind him. Apparently her shoes weren't quite as good in the slick conditions as she'd said.

Thomas decided to take the risk. He held out a gloved hand. "I'm wearing boots," he said. "If you hold my hand, we should make better time."

She stared at his hand for a second before slipping her mittened fingers into his. He gripped her hand firmly and focused again on getting them to the cottage without a fall.

The shrubs and plantings around the building had been transformed into rounded blobs of white, the rough edges softened with the snow. In spots, drifts had piled up, creating wide skirts on some of the bushes. In a few places, the wind had scoured away the snow and bare dirt or rock showed.

The walk to the cottage wasn't long, but they took it slow. When they reached the door of the stone cottage, Thomas let go of Poppy's hand and fumbled the key into the lock. Despite his gloves, his fingers were icy, while his face felt as if it were covered in fine scratches from the icy snow flung against it.

They rushed inside as soon as the door was open, both gasping in relief at being out of the weather. The foyer of the cottage had flagstone floors and a mat for scraping shoes. A row of pegs offered them a place for their coats, so they stripped out of them and hung them up to avoid trailing melting snow through the house. The cottage was colder than the main house, but it still felt pleasant after the walk over.

"Mrs. Bing?" Poppy called out, her voice ringing in the cottage.

No one answered, and Thomas wasn't surprised. There was something about the feel of the building that made him sure no one was there.

"We should still check out the rooms and maybe the surrounding area," Poppy said. "She could be here and unable to answer."

Thomas suspected that was a nicer way to say *dead*. When had he begun to expect dead bodies? "I believe the kitchen is straight ahead," he explained. "Off to the left is a shared living area, and the two suites are through that door." He waved toward it.

"I'll check the kitchen," Poppy said. "You do the living room, and then we'll search the suites together." She hurried off before he could come up with a good reason why they shouldn't separate. She was right. They should be efficient, and the place really did feel empty.

He walked into the living room. It had been several years since he'd been in the room, but it hadn't changed much. The furniture was of high quality, built to last but not overly ornamental. He thought the sofa had been reupholstered since he'd last seen it, but he wasn't sure. A large braided rug covered much of the floor, though it was well clear of the tiled hearth of a small fireplace. No fire burned in the grate, but a stack of wood nearby and a basket of wax-covered pine cones suggested a fire could be started quickly enough.

He wasn't surprised to hear Poppy from the doorway. "Kitchen's empty. Time for the suites. Do you know which is which?"

Thomas shook his head. "Though from how Cook was talking, I assume her door won't be locked."

"Good thinking." Poppy spun and headed for one of the doors, twisting the handle and opening it. "Voila, Cook's rooms."

The suite featured a small sitting room with one wall taken up by floor-to-ceiling bookcases. There was a mini fridge, and an electric teakettle sat on top of it. A love seat and one rocking chair provided the only seating, arranged neatly around a coffee table.

"Not here," Poppy said. She moved into the bedroom, and Thomas peered in after her. The bed had a wooden frame of the same kind of sturdy build as the rest of the furniture. A thick duvet covered the bed, and in one corner stood a tall chest of drawers. A pair of doors led to a closet hung with simple, casual clothes and a bathroom with a shower, but no tub.

"Bigger than my first apartment," Poppy observed. "And devoid of clues."

"Did you expect any?" Thomas asked.

"Not really, but you never know. Maybe in Mrs. Bing's rooms." She headed out of the suite and waited for Thomas to let them into the next rooms, which were locked as they'd expected. When they stepped inside, they found the suite to be a mirror image of Cook's. Searching didn't take long, and the contents weren't particularly different with one notable exception. On the coffee table in the sitting room sat a plant in a pot.

Poppy reached for it. "This plant has seen better days."

Thomas grabbed her wrist. "Don't touch it."

Poppy raised her eyebrows. "Why not?"

"I recognize the leaves," he said. "When I was writing the book about unique deaths in history, I researched a number of poisonous plants." He nodded toward the pot. "That's one of them."

"Really?" Poppy examined the plant without reaching out again. "What is it? Hemlock?"

"No, it's aconite."

"I've never heard of it."

"It's also called wolfsbane."

She stood up then, eyes wide. "Now I remember that part of the book. A guy accidentally poisoned himself because he thought he was a werewolf and was trying to cure himself."

"Right. He died from a heart attack brought on by the poison. Even handling the plant can cause a heart attack."

"That's uncomfortably coincidental considering Teddy's death had the appearance of a heart attack." Poppy gestured toward the plant on the table. "But if you were a poisoner, would you leave the murder weapon on your coffee table? Really, if Mrs. Bing is a diabolical murderer, you'd think she'd be sneakier about it."

"Murderers aren't always overly bright," Thomas said.

"But Mrs. Bing wasn't in the room with us when Teddy died, and Teddy poured the drink himself," Poppy insisted, "so how would she guess he was going to drink out of that glass."

"Could be she didn't care who drank out of it," Thomas said. "And we don't know that it was in the glass rather than the whiskey he drank."

Poppy winced. "That's dark. Any one of us might have consumed it by accident."

"You know," Thomas said. "I have to say I'm impressed with the way you've handled shock after shock since you arrived."

She reacted to the compliment with less enthusiasm than Thomas had hoped. "Because I'm a woman?"

"Hardly," he said. "You've met both my mother and my grandmother. Surely you realize I don't make a habit of underestimating women. But I have to assume most of your ghostwriting jobs are less eventful than this one."

"True enough." Then she brightened. "I can't say I mind the idea of being cut from the same cloth as your mother and your grandmother."

Thomas considered telling her that she probably would fit right into his family of beautiful, strong women, but decided that might be taken the wrong way. His estimation of her had been growing ever since he'd met her. If he could keep her and the other women in his life safe, he planned to tell her exactly how impressive she was.

"We should get back to the house," Poppy said. "Mrs. Bing isn't here. And that means she could be there."

"Let's go."

As they shrugged back into coats, Poppy held up the mittens again.

"These were a surprise. I expected Mariette to have some pricey leather gloves, but these are handmade. Does Mariette knit?"

Thomas shook his head. "My mother made them years ago. I believe Mariette has them mended every time they show wear."

Poppy held up her hand with the mitten on it. "Your grandmother never ceases to surprise me."

"It's her gift," Thomas said.

They made the return trip more quickly. Poppy didn't hesitate to slip her hand into his as soon as they stepped outside.

They found the others waiting in the foyer. "Has something new happened?" Thomas asked as he closed the door behind them.

"No, I was worried about you," Mariette said. "You took long enough. I assume you didn't find Mrs. Bing?"

"No, but we did find an unusual plant in her rooms," Thomas said. "Aconite. It's extremely poisonous."

"It causes heart attacks," Poppy added.

"You think the housekeeper killed Teddy?" Cecil asked. "We've fallen into a bad movie from the forties."

"We found the plant," Thomas said. "But we don't know that she used it. Mariette, what do you know about Mrs. Bing?"

"She's local," Mariette said. "But I don't know much beyond that. She had good references. She hasn't been with me long. I hired her when Mrs. Wiest retired in the fall. You remember her, don't you?"

"I do," Thomas said, though his recollection of the quiet, efficient woman was vague. He wasn't certain he'd ever had a conversation with her.

"She must have been ancient," Bethany said. "Mrs. Wiest was here forever. I loved her."

"And she loved you," Arthur said. "Nettie would have stayed on or come out of retirement if she'd known the young miss was actually coming home."

"Right, she always called me that." Bethany chuckled. "I remember insisting more than once that I wasn't so young anymore, but she'd only agree with me and go on about her work without changing." Then, as if the full ramifications of Arthur's words had finally sunk in, she raised her chin. "And I am not coming home, by the way. I came here to talk Mother out of her horrible plan to write this book."

"Good for you," Cecil said approvingly.

Mariette laughed. "I do believe that's the first time you two have ever agreed about anything."

Bethany's frown showed how little she was pleased by that thought.

"That plant," Cook said. "Does it mean I've been sharing the cottage with a murderer?"

"We don't know," Thomas said.

"All we really know is that she kept a deadly houseplant," Poppy added.

"A houseplant that could easily have been the murder weapon," Cecil cut in. "Meaning Mariette somehow invited a viper right into her household, and Teddy paid the price. Who knows? Maybe she bashed Jackie as well."

"Don't be ridiculous," Thomas said. "Cook and Mrs. Bing were in the cottage at the time."

"Unless the ghost I saw was Mrs. Bing going to the house to commit a murder," Cook said fretfully.

"No. Sorry, but it makes no sense," Poppy said, so firmly that she immediately had everyone's attention.

"Why?" Thomas asked.

"Because Jacqueline wasn't the first person to die," Poppy reminded them. "Matthew was. You said you hired Mrs. Bing after the previous housekeeper retired in the fall. In the time since you hired her, has Mrs. Bing been absent from the house for long enough to have made a trip to where Matthew lived?"

"Mrs. Bing hasn't left the island at all since I hired her," Mariette said. "She has time off, of course, but she has always been content to spend it reading or taking walks on the island. Though, of course, the walks decreased as the weather has grown colder."

"We don't know how long Matthew was dead," Cecil said. "Unless the detective told you, Mariette, and you didn't tell us."

"The police officer I spoke with on the phone didn't say, but I talked to Matthew on the phone less than a week ago," Mariette said. "And I know without question that Mrs. Bing hasn't left the island since then."

"Then she's not Matthew's killer," Thomas said. "And we don't know that she's anyone's killer. All we know is that she's missing, and we need to find her. I think we should try the upstairs after all. I believe we've reached the point where searching even the most unlikely places makes sense."

"In that case," Bethany said. "Shouldn't we check the secret passage?"

*E*veryone froze at Bethany's question, but Poppy recovered first. "What secret passage?"

Before Bethany could answer Poppy's question, Mariette cut in. "Don't be silly, Bethany. Mrs. Bing would hardly know about that dreadful closet your father built for you."

"You never approved of anything Dad did for me," Bethany said, taking a step toward her mother as her voice rose. "I'm surprised you let him remodel the lighthouse room for me."

"Can we table the sniping?" Thomas asked. "I would appreciate it if someone would explain what you're talking about."

"It's nothing," Mariette said dismissively. "When we first began building this house, Joseph wanted to connect the lighthouse keeper's cottage to the house. He felt it would make the building more useful in the winter."

"Wouldn't that have been nice to know about," Cook muttered, drawing a sharply disapproving expression from both Arthur and Mariette.

"It didn't happen because it ruined the design of the house, throwing it all out of balance. I put my foot down on that. He could drag me out to an isolated island with a baby, but at least the house had to suit me."

"How does that have anything to do with a secret passage?" Thomas asked. A question Poppy appreciated, since she was almost vibrating with curiosity ever since the words *secret passage* had been spoken.

"As I said," Mariette continued, "an annex was planned to connect the two buildings. It was even started. But it was never finished. Still a small section of the rockwork had been built, and rockwork isn't cheap. So we tore down most of the annex but left that bit of rockwork, simply closed it off to create an unused pocket."

"Then," Bethany jumped in. "Dad had that stone room opened up again when I was seven or eight. I told him the house needed a secret passage, so he gave me one. It's not really a passage—it's barely a room—but it does have a hidden door like you see in old movies and books."

"That room was impossible to keep clean. The inside walls aren't even properly finished. And with the bare rock, it's cold too," Mariette said.

"It was my favorite place when I was a child," Bethany said. "I made up so many stories and adventures there. Sometimes it was lonely being the lone kid on the island."

Mariette's face softened. "This can be a desolate place." Mother and daughter locked eyes, and some kind of understanding passed between them, if only the memory of shared emotion.

"Why did I never know about a secret room?" Thomas asked.

"Because the room hadn't been used in years, and it was filthy," Mariette said, drawing a huff from her daughter. "I was afraid you'd catch something in there. I would have had it walled up again, but Joseph would never agree to it. He could be astonishingly sentimental sometimes."

"Dad's been gone for a while now," Bethany said. "Did you get it walled up or have you become sentimental too?"

Mariette tried for her usual cool tone but didn't quite manage it. "I'm sure I would have gotten around to it."

"And you never went in there?" Thomas pressed.

Mariette raised her shoulder, "Perhaps once or twice, to be sure water wasn't seeping in."

Poppy kept hoping the wall between Mariette and Bethany was crumbling, but if it was, it wasn't coming down easily. And they still had to find Mrs. Bing. "Maybe we should check out this room."

"Why?" Mariette asked. "The housekeeper wouldn't have known anything about it unless Arthur told her."

"I did not, ma'am."

"She has to be somewhere," Thomas said. "And before we begin searching upstairs, it makes sense to check the one downstairs room we missed. If she is in there, it will open up a whole new line of inquiry."

"Be careful," Mariette said. "You're beginning to sound as if you've read entirely too many mystery novels."

"I'm trying to be logical," Thomas replied.

Mariette sniffed. "Fine. I think it's silly, but it won't do any harm." She waved a hand toward her daughter. "It's your room and your idea, so do you want to lead the way?"

"I do. It'll be nice to see the room again." Bethany headed from the drawing room, her chin raised in a gesture so like one her mother often used that it nearly made Poppy laugh. How could two women who were so much alike not notice they were?

Everyone followed Bethany as she moved quickly through the house, her ease with the building obvious. As she followed the group, Poppy again marveled at the thought of being a child in such a house, having a father who created secret passages and tower rooms for you. It must have been wonderful.

Finally Bethany stopped beside a wall, paneled in an ornate Georgian style. Bethany pressed on one corner of a recessed section of paneling, and a portion of the wall swung out easily. She grinned at the group. "Cool, right?"

Poppy peered past her and saw that the room beyond was quite small as Mariette had said. It was slightly larger than a closet, about the size of a comfortable powder room. The walls were stone and a wash of cold air came from inside. "Are there lights?"

"Of course," Bethany said. She reached around the doorway and flipped on the lights. "But if all of us go in there, it will be tight."

No one bothered to call out since it was clear Mrs. Bing was not in the small room. It was equally clear that Mariette's description of the room as filthy was incorrect. It was rough, but clean, beyond the clutter—a sign that someone had been in there recently. "We've had company," Thomas said, ducking around Bethany to step into the space. Poppy slipped by as well, curiosity burning in her.

A well-worn sleeping bag lay on the floor in a rumpled heap with a couple of blankets and a quilt. "I recognize those blankets and the quilt," Arthur said from the doorway. "They belong to Mrs. Winter."

"And now they're on the floor and some intruder has slept on them?" Mariette said, aghast. "We'll have to throw them out."

"Wouldn't washing suffice?" Bethany asked.

"I suppose, as long as I don't come into contact with them."

Bethany rolled her eyes and turned away from her mother, tapping her foot and staring down the hall as if watching for an intruder.

Mariette took advantage of her daughter's inattention to peek inside the room again, frown, and step inside. She picked up a small teddy bear from the floor and perched it carefully on one of the protruding rocks, then stepped out again.

Poppy watched the movement curiously. The teddy bear had probably been Bethany's, since the intruder would hardly have brought one in. Between the teddy bear and the mittens, Poppy realized Mariette was more sentimental than she let on.

Setting that thought aside to consider later, Poppy stepped closer to Thomas and peered around. Next to the sleeping bag was a bulging backpack. Thomas knelt to unzip it and pull out the contents onto the pile of bedding. It was stuffed with worn men's clothes.

"Unless Mrs. Bing has interesting taste in clothes, this backpack belongs to someone else." Thomas rose and held out a sweater. "Does anyone recognize this?"

"I have not seen it before," Arthur said, his face pinched with distaste.

"Nor have I," Mariette said. "Who has been trespassing in my home?"

"That is the question," Thomas agreed. "The police will want to see all of this, especially since it suggests another suspect if Jacqueline or Teddy were murdered."

"Is this someone you brought to the island?" Cecil demanded of Bethany.

"Me? Don't be stupid."

"You snuck onto the island," Cecil said. "Who's to say you didn't sneak someone on with you to be your hired assassin? Someone you told about this secret room? None of us knew about it."

"I knew about it," Mariette said.

"As did I," Arthur said. "And I should have been checking it regularly."

"I'll say," Cecil hissed, perfectly willing to share his ire with the group.

"Why would I suggest we come and check out this room if I'm the one who brought someone to stay in it?" Bethany asked. Poppy considered that a completely reasonable question. Clearly no one had thought of the room, so why bring it up if Bethany was hiding someone there? It made no sense.

"Maybe you had a falling-out with your accomplice," Cecil said. "Or simply decided to throw him to the wolves to save yourself now that you've been dragged out of hiding."

"No one dragged me anywhere."

Cecil shook his fist at Bethany. "I demand you tell us who your accomplice is and why you are killing people."

"I told you," Bethany said. "It has nothing to do with me."

"Liar."

"Cecil, stop!" Mariette shouted. "Or I will have Arthur knock you down."

Cecil narrowed his eyes at her. "As if he could. Don't think you're in the clear either, Mariette. You are the one who brought us all here to die."

"Cecil," Thomas said. "You will calm down right now, or Arthur and I will restrain you for your own good and the good of us all."

"You wouldn't dare," Cecil said, but Poppy could tell from his voice that he knew they absolutely would. He held out a bit longer but eventually took a step back. "Fine, but you'd better sort out what's going on."

"That has been my goal since all of this started," Thomas said.

Cecil didn't make any more demands, but he did glare accusingly at everyone around him.

Thomas surveyed the rest of the group. "Does anyone else have any ideas?"

"Maybe someone stowed away on your boat without your knowledge," Cook suggested to Bethany.

"The boat isn't nearly big enough for that," Bethany said.

"Since I didn't know about this room," Thomas said, "who all did?"

"Arthur, of course, and me," Mariette said. "And Bethany. And the workmen who built it. I have no idea what could have happened to them. They wouldn't be young men, if they're even still alive."

"There could be a *few* others," Bethany said. When everyone turned toward her, she shrugged. "Of course I told other kids. I was a child, and having a secret passage was cool."

"So it could have been most anyone from the village?" Cecil asked. "How helpful. How's your relationship with the village, Mariette?"

Mariette didn't answer.

"I'm not sure we're accomplishing anything," Poppy said. "I know I'm so tired I can barely think, and I imagine we're all feeling that way."

"She has a point," Bethany said. "We can't exactly go out and search the island for Mrs. Bing or this mysterious interloper—not in the middle of the night during a storm."

"Perhaps not," Thomas said. "But we can search the upstairs. I don't think any of us should lower our guard before we do that."

Poppy struggled to rally. "I'm in."

"No, you're not," Thomas said. "You're actually swaying. I will go upstairs and search with Arthur and Cecil. You, Cook, Mariette, and my mother should wait down here."

"We will wait in the drawing room," Mariette said. "The fire is probably still burning, and if not, it can be stirred to life again. And we'll have comfortable seating there."

"If the four of you stay together, I think you should be safe enough," Thomas said. "The fireplace tools would make formidable weapons if anyone tries to hurt you. In the meanwhile, we'll search as fast as I can."

"What if I prefer not to waste time and energy wandering around upstairs?" Cecil asked.

"I'm not leaving you alone with the women," Thomas said. "But we could tie you up."

Cecil flinched. "Fine. Let's get this imbecilic charade going."

"After we get the women to the drawing room," Thomas said.

"Thomas," Mariette said. "We're not crossing a wasteland. We're walking to the drawing room in my own house. I think we'll make it."

"Really, Thomas," Bethany said. "Give us some credit."

Thomas must have been stunned by the rare unity between mother and daughter because he didn't argue. "Then we will meet you in the drawing room once we've checked the upstairs."

As the group divided, Poppy couldn't help but think that splitting up never ended well in any horror movie she'd ever watched, but she didn't think that would be helpful commentary, and she really didn't have the energy to join the search. In fact, once they were in the warm drawing room, she sank into a comfortable love seat and immediately fell asleep.

She woke with a start as Cook shook her shoulder. "Time for bed, Miss."

She blinked and looked around for Thomas. Not surprisingly, he stood face-to-face with Cecil near the door to the drawing room. "I merely asked if there were other hidden rooms," Cecil grumbled. "I prefer not to be murdered by a killer hiding behind another secret panel."

"If there are any other hidden rooms, I don't know about them," Bethany said.

"Nor do I," Mariette said. "And I would. Joseph and I discussed every inch of this building. The only reason we have one hidden room is to suit a little girl's whims."

"You could stop blaming me anytime now, Mother," Bethany said, and Poppy's heart sank at hearing mother and daughter fighting again.

On impulse, Poppy said, "What was that teddy bear you picked up in the hidden room, Mariette?"

"Teddy bear?" Bethany repeated.

"It was simply an old toy Bethany left in there," Mariette said. "I didn't care for the thought of some intruder touching our things."

"Was it Teddums?" Bethany asked. "Have you kept Teddums all this time?"

Mariette dithered a moment, then said. "How would I know which toy it was? You had so many."

"I'm going to bed now," Cecil cut in sharply. "I'll be taking a heavy walking stick with me, so I suggest no one try to come into my room."

"Locking the door should be sufficient," Thomas said. "But I agree that we should go upstairs now. We'll go as a group and check each room before leaving anyone alone in it."

"I'll appreciate that," Cook said. "All of this is hard on the nerves. I'm not sure I'll sleep a wink."

"I recommend you do," Arthur told her. "You'll have meals to make tomorrow."

Poppy rose to her feet, her body sore from napping in the awkward position, though at least she felt less sluggish from exhaustion.

"Is everyone going to walk up the lighthouse stairs with me?" Bethany asked. "Since my room is up there."

"Not anymore," Thomas said. "There's no way to lock anyone out of the tower. You can take one of the upstairs rooms."

"I believe you can have your choice," Mariette said. "There's Teddy's room, Jacqueline's room, and the room Arthur made up for Mrs. Bing."

The defiant expression Bethany had been wearing since Poppy had found her slipped away. "The poor woman. Do you think she's outside in the snow?"

"If she is, I'd like to know why," Thomas said.

"That will be difficult to get out of her," Cecil observed, "since spending the night out in the snow would probably be fatal."

"Don't be so macabre, Cecil," Mariette said peevishly.

"She could have gone down to the boathouse," Bethany suggested. "Even if the boat is out of order, the building would offer some shelter."

"We'll find out tomorrow," Mariette said.

"You can have my room, Mother," Thomas said, drawing the topic back to rooms. "If you want. I'm not planning to sleep much anyway."

"Who cares what room she sleeps in. Can we go?" Cecil demanded. "I want to sleep."

And so they went, trooping out of the room and up the stairs with dull, shuffling steps. Poppy wasn't sure if it was simply exhaustion that had them acting like a parade of sleepwalkers, or if the gloom of what had been happening weighed each person down.

As she trudged up each step, her hand lightly grazing the banister, she wondered if one person was feeling the weight more than the others. The discovery that some unidentified person had been staying in the house in secret didn't mean none of the people around her were involved. The thought made her feel unsafe, but she found she couldn't push it away.

Great. I probably won't sleep a wink. But she intended to try. She only hoped the effort didn't kill her. Literally.

$\mathcal{A}$s the door to his grandmother's room closed and he heard the lock click into place, Thomas took deep breaths, hoping to relieve the tension building in him. He reminded himself that they were safe. And that he wouldn't let anyone in their rooms.

"You are welcome to sleep in my room, sir," Arthur said. "I can retrieve a cot from the attic to sleep on myself. If you don't mind sharing."

"Thank you, Arthur," Thomas said. "But a cot won't be necessary. I prefer that you and I take shifts keeping watch over this floor. I'm not sure the killer is done, not while Cecil and Mariette are still alive. When I'm not on watch, I'll nap on the chaise in Teddy's room."

Arthur nodded his head ponderously. "That would be wise."

Thomas noticed that Arthur's lined face was gray and his eyes were bloodshot. He didn't need to be up all night. "I'll take the first watch," Thomas said. "I'm too keyed up to sleep right now anyway. Go on to bed, and I'll wake you in a few hours."

"Of course." As Arthur shuffled toward his room, Thomas realized his evaluation must be right. Arthur would have offered at least token resistance if he weren't completely exhausted.

Thomas debated his next move. Should he stay on the floor with everyone and merely pace the length of the hall, or should he patrol the entire house?

Weariness was slowing his decision-making, and he was still trying to pick a plan when a door opened and Poppy stepped out into the hall. Her hair was slightly tousled, and she'd changed her clothes.

She wore a dark sweatshirt with the word *Writer* printed on it in fading, almost ghostly white letters and dark knit pants. She'd shucked off her shoes and stood in the hall in slippers. "I caught a second wind," she said, ruefully. "I'm wide awake. The nap in the sitting room is probably the culprit."

"Nice outfit," he said.

She looked down sharply, as if she'd forgotten what she was wearing. Her face reddened. "The shirt was a present from a friend. She thought it was funny."

He hadn't been teasing about the outfit. He enjoyed this comfortable version of Poppy. "I don't suppose you have any insights to share about all of this," Thomas said as she approached him.

"I wish," Poppy said. "But I think your mother and Mariette are softening. Maybe they'll reach a détente."

"That would be nice. It's not easy being 'man in the middle' between two people you love."

"No, I'd imagine not. I'm sure they appreciate it, though."

"You think?" He chuckled. She was an optimist. He could use more optimism.

She dimpled in response. "I do."

Not for the first time, Thomas was struck by how pretty Poppy was. Her eyes were full of whatever she was feeling, which probably made her a terrible liar. He appreciated being around someone without a trace of guile. It was novel.

He leaned toward her, and he might even have taken the chance and kissed her if they hadn't both been distracted by a thumping sound over their heads.

"What's up there?" Poppy whispered.

"An attic," Thomas said. "An empty attic."

"Maybe not so empty. Can we get up there?"

"This way." He took Poppy's hand without thinking and was surprised when she didn't jerk it away from him. Together they hurried quietly down the hall. Thomas envied Poppy's soft-soled slippers, which let her move in near silence.

They reached the end of the hall, and Thomas eased open the door to the attic stairs and started up, reluctantly letting go of Poppy's hand so they could hold the handrail along the steep attic steps.

When they'd nearly reached the top, the upper door burst open and a stout man thundered down the stairs. Thomas had no time to prepare, and the man slammed past him, using his greater weight to muscle Thomas out of the way.

Thomas's boot missed the step when he was knocked backward, and he fell into Poppy, who was already struggling to stay on her feet after the intruder passed. They were saved from tumbling all the way down the stairs by the narrowness of the space. Thomas caught the railing and twisted, desperate not to be the one who seriously hurt Poppy.

Wide-eyed and gasping, she clung to the railing behind him, a few steps lower than she'd been.

"Are you all right?" he asked. "Did I hurt you?"

"I'm fine." She was already pivoting to head down the stairs. "We have to go after him."

Thomas hurried after her, but when they reached the floor below, there was no sign of anyone in the hall. "How did he manage that?" Poppy demanded. "We were right behind him."

"He was moving pretty fast," Thomas said. "But he may be in one of these rooms."

"Then we need to find him."

Thomas knocked on the first door they came to, and Cook opened it to peer out at them. "What's all that clattering?"

"You heard someone?"

"I did," she confirmed. "Sounded like he was dragging a cow down the hall."

A door opened further along, and Mariette stepped out, her face shiny with moisturizer. "What's going on?"

"Did you hear someone run by?" Poppy asked.

"I did. Was that the two of you?"

"No," Thomas said. "Someone was in the attic."

Cook yelped. "Was it the killer?"

"I don't know. But if you heard him run past, he could be in the next wing," Thomas and Poppy continued on, with Cook and Mariette adding to the parade down the hall.

They crossed the landing, and Poppy peered over the rail. "I don't see anyone moving downstairs," she said. "But if he slid down the rail, he could have had time to get out of sight."

"You think he slid down the rail?" Thomas said, incredulous.

She shrugged. "It's what I would have done."

Thomas wasn't certain. "We need to check on the others."

"He could have gone after Bethany!" Mariette headed for the next wing. "Bethany?"

Three doors opened at Mariette's sharp yell. Bethany stuck her head out of Thomas's room. "Mother?" she said. "Are you all right?"

"I'm fine."

"What is going on?" Cecil demanded. "I thought we were supposed to be getting some sleep."

"Poppy and I heard a sound from the attic," Thomas said. "When we went to investigate, we were almost knocked down the attic stairs by a stranger."

"Did you recognize him?" Cecil asked.

Thomas didn't answer immediately, gathering his thoughts. His impression of the man was fleeting, but the man had been dressed in layers of dusty rags with something pulled over his head. A sack? A pillowcase? A rip in one side offered only the smallest slit for the man to see, but apparently that was enough to allow him to get away.

"He had his head covered," Thomas said. "Poppy, did you notice anything about him?"

"It happened so fast, and I couldn't see him clearly," Poppy admitted. "He smelled, though. I think it was the scent of mothballs."

Thomas filed that impression before refocusing on the group forming in the hall. "He ran past the rooms in that wing. Did you hear him come through here?"

"I didn't," Bethany said, "but I was asleep. I sat down for a minute before getting changed for bed and I fell asleep right in the chair."

"I was sleeping too," Cecil said. "And I would prefer sleeping to whatever we are doing now."

Everyone ignored him.

"I heard nothing," Arthur said. "But I was asleep as well. I'm sorry."

"You don't have to be sorry for getting well-deserved rest," Mariette said. "That's what bedtime is for. Shall we search for the intruder?"

"No," Thomas said. "*We* shall not. You should all go to bed and get some sleep. I can search, though I wouldn't be surprised if he took this opportunity to leave the house entirely."

"I don't really want to sleep alone anymore," Cook said, twisting her hands.

"I'll be honest," Bethany said. "The idea doesn't appeal to me either." She gave her mother a grudging smile. "I don't suppose I could share with you, could I? As tired as I am, we could probably manage without fighting too much."

"I have no desire to fight with you," Mariette said, and sincerity showed in the softening of her face. "You're welcome to share with me. We should get as much sleep as we can before dawn."

"I do not need a sleep companion," Cecil said, "and I do not want to do any more searching either." And with that, he stomped to his room, slamming the door behind him.

"You're welcome to share with me," Poppy said to Cook. "My room is nearly as big as my whole apartment at home."

"Thank you, Miss," Cook said. "I'll get some blankets and pillows from my room to make a pallet on the floor."

"That's not necessary," Thomas said. "Arthur said there's a cot in the attic. Isn't that right?"

"Yes sir," the butler said. "I will go and get it."

"No. You stay here and watch over Cook and Poppy. I'll go get it."

"I don't need a guardian," Poppy said.

"I don't mind it," Cook chimed in. "I don't think of myself as cowardly, but this job has been a lot."

"Arthur will guard Cook," Poppy said. "I'll come with you, Thomas. Maybe we can figure out what the intruder was doing up there."

"Fine," Thomas said, though it was anything but fine. He hated the thought of putting Poppy in danger again. He shouldn't have done it the first time. But at least if she was with him, he could protect her—or try anyway. "You can come with me to get the cot, but afterward, I expect you to lock yourself in your room with Cook. You will not come with me when I search downstairs."

Poppy grinned at him. "We'll see. Hold on a second." She ran into her room and came out with a flashlight. "Let's go finish what we started." She didn't wait for a response, already heading toward the attic door.

Thomas hurried after her, wondering if it was his lot in life to be ordered around by strong-willed women.

Weariness draped around Poppy like a heavy blanket as she strode down the hall, but she doubted she'd be able to sleep if she left Thomas alone to do the dangerous tasks he set for himself, so she pushed past it, hoping it didn't show. It wasn't as if she saw herself as some kind of superhero. In truth, she longed for an end to the scary night and would welcome the arrival of the police in the morning if the storm broke. Surely it was blowing itself out by the hour.

She shook off her wandering thoughts. She would need to focus if she didn't want to make mistakes. When she reached the open door of the attic stairs, she headed up, assuming that Thomas was right behind her, probably annoyed that she'd taken the lead.

At the top of the stairs, the second door hung open as well, and the space beyond was ominously dark. But the intruder had already left. There was no need to be scared anymore, so she began the climb.

"Poppy," Thomas said. "Hold up."

She didn't. The stairs were too narrow for Thomas to pass her easily so she decided to hurry to the attic where they'd have more room to stand together. Once in the attic, she held up her flashlight and pressed the button. The beam wasn't as bright as she'd prefer, but it showed her a dangling string several feet away. She tugged on it as Thomas joined her. The weak light bulb offered more illumination than her small flashlight, but not by much.

"You didn't need to run off and leave me," Thomas said.

"You're considerably taller than me. I didn't think catching up would be a problem."

"Are you always so stubborn?"

Poppy thought about the question, wanting to answer it fairly. "Yes." She lifted her chin to meet his eyes, careful not to aim the flashlight into his face. In the dim light, his face was full of shadows. "Do you prefer women who are more pliant?"

"Only when I'm concerned they'll get themselves killed." He scanned the attic, leaning to see into darker places. "I'm not entirely sure where the cot is stored."

The attic around them had the sloped ceiling of most attics. The roof beams were not exposed. The ceiling featured some kind of beaded paneling. The room wasn't so full that it was difficult to move around, but there were pieces of cast-off furniture, a few trunks, and some more shadowy things in the corners. It was also relatively clean.

If Poppy hadn't already seen how clean the secret passage had been, she would have found the lack of heavy dust in the attic surprising. "Who dusts up here?"

"Mrs. Bing maybe," Thomas said.

"Then who cleaned the secret room?" Poppy asked.

"Excuse me?"

"It was clean inside the secret room. Sure, there were things scattered on the floor, but those rock walls should have been visibly dirty, as should the floor. It wasn't. Someone had cleaned the room recently."

"Must have been Arthur."

"It's worth asking when we're done here." Poppy headed for one of the darker corners, assuming that the cot must be hidden in the shadows since it was not amongst the better-lit furniture.

"Why do you suppose the intruder was up here?" Poppy asked as she shifted some old framed paintings and found nothing but some small boxes behind them.

"Hiding possibly," Thomas said. "I don't see anything obviously disturbed."

"I wonder," Poppy said. "That man stank of mothballs. I suspect that smell came from one of these trunks." She walked over and opened one. It contained what she guessed were old drapes, carefully folded.

The smell of mothballs wafted up from it, but the contents of the chest didn't appear to have been gone through.

Thomas opened another chest. "That bag over his head suggests he was someone we would recognize."

"Maybe," Poppy said, leaning over his shoulder to peer in. More folded fabrics. "Or he didn't want us to give a clear description to the police."

"Over there," Thomas said.

Poppy spun so fast she nearly lost her balance, immediately alarmed. But Thomas was indicating the cot, visible from their new position. *If I don't end up scared to death by the end of this, it'll be a miracle.*

They hauled the cot over to the stairs, but before they started down, Thomas laid a gentle hand on Poppy's arm. "Are you okay? I mean, really okay? I slammed into you pretty hard on the stairs earlier."

"I really am fine," she said. "It was actually less awkward to bump into you on the stairs than it was to slap you on the dock."

Thomas laughed out loud. "I'm surprised you have the energy for jokes."

"I always have the energy to enjoy the absurdity of life." As they were standing right under the light, Poppy could see the warmth in Thomas's eyes.

"Good attitude. You're an impressive woman, Poppy Hayes."

"You're saying that because you're afraid of being smacked again."

Again he laughed, but he also moved closer, and Poppy wondered if he was about to kiss her. She'd thought he was going to earlier, but it hadn't happened. She was beginning to think she would have to go ahead and kiss him when the horror of the weekend was over.

"Are you two coming down?" Mariette called up the stairs, and Thomas immediately stepped away from Poppy.

"Did something happen?" he asked.

"We're all eager to get to bed," Bethany answered. "Could you two flirt later?"

Poppy saw the back of Thomas's neck darken. Was the man blushing? She tried to creep around without him noticing so she could see his face.

But Thomas moved too quickly, hauling the cot downstairs. "Poppy, will you please shut off the overhead light?"

"No problem." As the dark settled around her, she followed as closely behind Thomas as was safe. She'd had enough visits to creepy places for one night. Then she remembered Thomas was going to check downstairs again and she groaned softly. Maybe a few more creepy places were in store for her.

Thomas set up the cot in Poppy's room, and Cook piled it with blankets and pillows she'd collected from her own room. "The snow has stopped," Cook said. "I saw stars out the window while you two were gone. The police will be here in the morning. Then everything will be okay." She sounded so happy at the thought that a cold weight settled in Poppy's stomach. In scary movies, didn't the worst things always happen right after someone announced that it was all over?

14

When morning dawned, they discovered the blizzard had blown itself out. Sunlight streamed through the windows of Poppy's room and nudged her awake. She swung her legs over the edge of the bed and leaned forward to speak to Cook. But Cook was gone, and the blankets and pillow were stacked neatly on the cot. "I guess I was really out of it," Poppy said.

She had some excuse. She'd all but sleepwalked through the search of the downstairs rooms for the intruder, but even so, it had taken a while. Then Thomas had insisted on checking the lighthouse room—a decision that had nearly made Poppy whimper—but they'd found nothing and eventually headed upstairs to the bedrooms. Cook was sound asleep and snoring lightly when Poppy crept in. Within seconds of crawling into her own bed, Poppy had fallen into deep, dreamless sleep.

And now it's time to get moving. Poppy retrieved her phone from under her pillow. It could use recharging, and service would certainly be spotty at best—still, she hadn't wanted to be too far from it during the night. With it safely in hand, she hopped off the bed and tapped on the bathroom door in case Cook was in there, but the room was empty.

She showered and dressed in another of her collection of cozy sweaters, matched with a pair of brown wool slacks and boots. She guessed they'd be outside later and didn't want to tromp through snow in her shoes again. Her pixie-cut hair didn't need any special grooming, so she left her rooms, wondering if she would be the last one downstairs. *What happened to moving as a group?* Of course, nothing was ever as scary with the sun shining. She hoped the dose of courage wouldn't get anyone hurt.

Poppy headed first for the dining room, but when she found the room empty, she walked through to the kitchen and discovered she was last to come down after all. Other than Mrs. Bing, who was still absent.

The large kitchen was busy with Cook splitting her time between checking on a rack of bacon under the broiler of one oven and pulling a large pan of French toast from the other one. Arthur stood beside Thomas at one counter where Arthur was making coffee in a French press while Thomas filled a teapot.

All the activity made Poppy feel guilty.

"Sorry I'm late," Poppy said.

"Don't worry yourself," Mariette called from the round staff dining table. The elegant woman Poppy had met on the first day was more rumpled, and the dark circles under her eyes, emphasized by the white turban over her hair, suggested she would have benefited from the sleep Poppy had gotten. "I heard you and Thomas go down to hunt for the intruder," Mariette continued. "You were probably dead on your feet by the time you got to bed."

Poppy managed not to wince at the idiom. Somehow any use of the word *dead* felt insensitive. She surveyed the room. "Can I help with anything?"

Arthur appraised her. She couldn't say what he was checking for, but his tone was doubtful when he spoke. "You may set the table if you like, since we seem to be quite casual today." Poppy noticed the tall butler had skipped his more formal clothing in favor of jeans and a pullover sweater, which appeared to be the uniform of the day. Thomas wore something strikingly similar.

Trying not to take offense at Arthur's obvious judgment of her cooking skills, Poppy simply set to work gathering dishes and silverware from the sideboard near where Thomas made up a tea tray. It was good to be doing something, though Mariette, Bethany, and Cecil clearly didn't agree, since they sat around the staff table and waited for their food.

When the food was ready, they all settled together at the table. The seating was tight despite their depleted numbers, but they made do. The time for being picky about the distinction between staff and employer had passed, at least in Poppy's opinion.

At least the food hadn't suffered from the situation. The French toast was fluffy and the bacon perfectly crisp.

"Have you called the police yet?" Poppy asked, peering around the group. "They'll probably want an update."

"Not yet," Mariette stood slowly, in visible pain. "I wanted some food before I faced the chaos that is sure to follow such a call." She crossed to the landline phone that hung on the wall and lifted the handset from the holder. She punched some buttons, held it to her ear, and frowned. "The phone is dead. I suppose that's no great surprise in light of the storm. Considering the police already knew about Jacqueline, I'm sure they'll be here as soon as they can."

"Did anyone tell them that she may have been murdered?" Poppy asked.

"No." Mariette hung up the kitchen phone and held out her hand. "Thomas, let me use your cell phone. Poppy's right. They need to be updated."

Thomas shook his head. "Sorry, but it's upstairs. I didn't see it when I first woke up, and then I forgot about it. I suppose I'm still tired."

No one had their phone with them except Poppy, who didn't enjoy being too far from her electronic security blanket. She often used her phone to take photos or make recordings when she worked, so she was rarely far from it.

Poppy hadn't tried to make a call from the phone since she'd arrived, and she checked the screen to find the tiniest sliver of a bar. "I'm not sure I have enough signal to make a call, but you're welcome to use it." She passed it over to Mariette.

"That's what happens when you live on an island," Bethany said. "Even with all my parents' money, cell reception here can be spotty at best."

As Poppy had feared, Mariette was unable to get through. "There's a cell tower right outside the village, so we usually get better reception than this. I don't understand it. The storm is over."

"The storm could have caused problems with the tower," Thomas said. "I know they'll be here eventually, but since they don't know Jacqueline's death is suspicious or about anything that has happened since, we may not be a priority. Especially if they have other storm-related incidents. Maybe someone should get my mother's rental boat and go to the mainland to contact the police."

"I can go," Bethany said.

"No," her mother responded. "The water will still be choppy. I don't want you taking risks."

Poppy braced for an argument between the two women, but Bethany gently touched her mother's hand. "You really don't have to worry. We're going to be fine."

"I am going to search outside for the housekeeper," Thomas announced. "If I can't find Mrs. Bing, I'll take the boat to the mainland and update the police. If I do find her, I may need to take her with me for immediate treatment, especially if she was out in the storm."

"That's a good plan," Cecil said. "You go, and Mariette can keep trying to get through while you're gone."

Bethany set down the cup of coffee she'd been staring into. "Why does having you agree with Thomas's plan immediately convince me it's a bad one?"

"Because you're paranoid," Cecil said.

"Stop it, both of you," Mariette said sharply. "Thomas, you go find Mrs. Bing, then get the boat and the police. I'll keep trying to make the call. Arthur will be here to keep us safe."

Poppy feared Mrs. Bing could be beyond treatment if she were out in the storm, but she spoke up. "I'll come with you, Thomas. You shouldn't be outside on your own."

Thomas raised both eyebrows. "So you'll be my bodyguard?"

"Maybe," Poppy said. "Or else I'll run screaming for help if we run into trouble. I can scream really loud. The police would probably hear me from the mainland."

The joke made him smile. "In that case, I appreciate the company."

Though the temperature outside was far from comfortable, the lack of wind or falling snow gave the illusion of warmth. When they stepped into the occasional pool of sunshine, both Thomas and Poppy raised their faces to the sky in unison, like sunflowers bathing in the tiny rush of warmth.

Poppy was dressed in her own coat and knit hat and had become the trim, almost magical creature Thomas had seen at the dock when she'd arrived. Was it really such a short time ago since he'd first seen the pert, trim figure with her back to him? He felt as if they'd been at the house for weeks, waiting through the storm.

Snow crunched under their boots, as they circled the large house, hunting for Mrs. Bing.

"I would have been fine to do this alone," Thomas said. He carried a walking stick he'd retrieved from the umbrella stand near the front door. It wasn't an impressive weapon, but it was better than nothing.

"I don't doubt it," Poppy said. "But I'd have been left inside worrying. So I'm doing this for entirely selfish reasons."

"You're out in the cold for selfish reasons?" Thomas said.

"You got it." Poppy beamed at him, and Thomas found he couldn't look away from the glow. How had he gotten so smitten with the woman so quickly?

"What?" Poppy asked. "You're staring at me funny again."

"Sorry. It seems my face does that sometimes." He forced himself to peer past her along the wall. "What's that?"

Poppy followed his line of sight. "Near the shrubs?"

"Behind them."

They crunched through the snow to the dark patch near the bushes. "A shutter came off one of the windows," Thomas said. "Half-buried in snow that way, it was hard to tell what it was." He shielded his eyes with his arm and examined the side of the house. "It must have come from the second floor. See? I think that's one of the bathrooms."

"Yep," Poppy said. "Should we dig it out?"

"Not now. We need to focus on covering ground." They skirted the shrubs and left the shutter behind them.

Poppy hunched her shoulders as the chill breeze the house had been blocking hit them. "I've been thinking about the intruder last night. Do you think that guy is the one who killed Matthew? Then maybe he came to the island and started killing people here."

Thomas wished he had an answer. "I don't know. If that's true, I can't guess why."

"How much do you know about your grandparents' business?" Poppy asked. "I mean I guess it's your family business too, right?"

"Not really. My business is teaching at the college. And my mother has never been connected to the family business either. It was strictly Mariette and my grandfather, and they were never forthcoming about details."

"From what Mariette and I have discussed for the book so far, it's possible the business was tied to some bad things. But that still doesn't explain Matthew. According to Mariette, he was the holdout, the good guy in the group."

"He was still part of the group," Thomas reminded her. "But I don't know. None of this makes sense to me. If it did, I would have had a better idea of what we should do."

"Now that we're out here," Poppy said, changing the subject. "I wish I'd brought my phone. I could keep trying to make the call. It's possible there are spots on the island that still get reception. I've experienced that in remote places before."

"Maybe, but I suspect the problem is the village cell tower."

"Do you think it's odd that no one had their phones this morning?" Poppy asked. "People are glued to their phones these days."

"Not so much out here," Thomas said. "If it weren't for the terrible things that have happened, my lack of phone would be almost a relief. Sometimes we're too connected by modern technology."

"I suppose," Poppy said as they rounded the next corner, completing their lap around the house. "Where to now? We could circle the lighthouse keeper's cottage."

"Or check inside it again," Thomas suggested. "It would have been a good place for the intruder to get out of the storm, once we'd flushed him from the attic."

So they tromped through the snow. Once again, Thomas could see the wet snow soaking through the bottom of his pant legs, and the chill was finally sinking into his feet through the boots. It wasn't as bad as it had been, but it would be nice to go inside the cottage for a minute.

They found the door to the lighthouse keeper's cottage ajar. Thomas put his finger to his lips and held up his hand for Poppy to stop and wait. She didn't argue. He crept into the cottage. Signs of recent passage were visible in the common rooms, from muddy tracks to open cupboards in the kitchen and even a smoldering fire in the fireplace. He'd been right. The intruder had sheltered in the cottage for the night.

He shook his head in annoyance. He should have gone to the cottage again when they didn't find the intruder in the house, but he'd been so tired, and he'd seen Poppy was in even worse shape.

He checked both suites and found that Cook's bed was rumpled and the quilt stained with mud. The intruder had come and gone.

Thomas opened the front door and found Poppy hugging herself and stomping her feet. "Did you find anything?" she asked, teeth chattering.

"Someone was in here after our search," he said.

"Mrs. Bing?"

"I don't think so." Mrs. Bing would probably have slept in her own bed, and it was unlikely that the housekeeper would have left such a mess. "I think we need to go and find my mother's boat. We need to bring the police now."

"Sounds good to me."

They left the manicured area around both buildings and started down the path toward the boathouse. The cove where Thomas had spent countless happy hours swimming when he was a kid visiting the island was best reached from a spot off the boathouse path. Of course, with the icy snow, the route would be treacherous. The snow hid plenty of tripping hazards.

That was made clear when they started downhill toward the boat launch and Poppy managed to step off the partially hidden path and into a hole. She pitched forward with a yelp.

Thomas caught her before she hit the ground. He held her close to steady her, and to reassure himself as much as her. "Careful," he said, reluctantly helping her stand by herself again. "We've had enough tumbles."

Poppy's already chill-reddened cheeks darkened more. "Sorry about that."

"No apology necessary," he said. *You've been the bright spot in this whole search.* He held out a hand. "We should probably hold onto one another again. The path gets steeper from here."

Poppy slipped her hand into his. "Good idea."

Despite the demanding path, Thomas found he was enjoying the morning far more than he'd have thought, even with his annoyance at having missed the intruder in the lighthouse keeper's cottage. The house had become almost oppressive during the storm, so despite the cold and his worries about the intruder, he still managed to enjoy being outside with a lovely woman holding his hand.

The pleasant thought ended abruptly when Thomas slipped and skidded downhill for a couple of yards. He released Poppy's hand immediately to avoid pulling her down with him.

"Thomas? Are you all right?" Poppy called when he stopped the slide by grabbing a thin tree.

The new vantage point showed him something he hadn't been able to see from the path. Up ahead, someone had dragged a few branches into a pile, possibly hoping snow would turn the pile into more bumps in the landscape. But the snow had not quite completed the job. Instead, Thomas could see several tufts of hair and a glimpse of a face through the branches. "I found something," Thomas called, though he hadn't said it as loudly as he'd intended, so he cleared his throat and raised his voice. "The way down is treacherous. Wait there."

Using the tree for support, he carefully swung himself closer to the piled branches. He had to be sure. From the new angle, he was able to see the housekeeper's body a little better—well enough to spot the knife buried in her chest.

Mrs. Bing was dead.

*W*ith Mrs. Bing beyond help, Thomas carefully made his way up the hill, not wanting to disturb the body. His first priority had to be getting the police to the island, and that meant finding his mother's boat.

"What is it?" Poppy asked as she held out a hand to help him over the last slippery ground. "What did you find?"

"Mrs. Bing. She was murdered."

"Are you sure it wasn't an accident?"

"I doubt she accidentally stabbed herself in the chest." At Poppy's expression, he felt bad about his bluntness. "We need to get to my mother's boat."

"What? No. We have to go and tell everyone about Mrs. Bing."

"Why?" Thomas said. "They can't help her. None of us can help her, and we need to get the police."

"Your mother and grandmother will want to know," Poppy said. "And if you can't see that's the right thing to do, then you go ahead and find your mother's boat. I'll go and give everyone the bad news about Mrs. Bing." She started up the path immediately, apparently not open to discussing it.

"No," he said, catching her by the arm. "We can't separate, not with clear proof there's a killer out here."

"I am telling them about Mrs. Bing," Poppy said.

"Fine. We'll go let them know, then I'll go out again. I have to get to the boat. We need the police here. No one is safe until they arrive."

The walk to the house was quiet, with both of them obviously unhappy with the exchange they'd had. He followed Poppy's straight back as she headed toward the house. She barely watched her feet but managed to pick the best spots to step all the same. At least if she slipped from the way she was marching along, he'd be in a position to catch her.

They reached the more level part of the path with a few minor slips and no damage. Thomas wished the same could be said for the housekeeper. He thought of the fearful woman and wondered what had gotten her outside where she could be killed. Maybe the intruder had found her alone in the hall and dragged her outside with him. But if so, why kill her so far from the house? Besides, he'd noticed that she was wearing a coat and boots. Would a kidnapper really let her get practical clothes if the plan was to take her outside and kill her?

The questions that ran through his head kept him busy until they reached the house. The door swung open while they were still stamping snow from their boots. Mariette greeted them triumphantly and waved them through the door. "I'm glad you two didn't leave. I reached the police on Poppy's phone. They're already on their way."

She held out the phone, and Poppy took it before shrugging out of her coat. "That's good news," Poppy said, though her voice was flat.

"We didn't make it to the boat," Thomas added. "We found Mrs. Bing. She wasn't far from the boathouse, but well off the path. She's been killed."

Mariette's posture drooped immediately. "The poor girl. What on earth was she doing outside?"

"I don't know," Thomas said. "She was dressed for the weather, but I couldn't tell much more. I didn't want to disturb the body."

Mariette's expression grew hopeful. "Are you sure she was dead?

Maybe she passed out or something. If she was dressed warmly enough to survive the cold, we should go get her."

"No, Mariette," Thomas kept his voice as gentle as he could. His grandmother had weathered so many shocks, and he was beginning to seriously fear for her health. "She was stabbed."

"Oh." Mariette swayed on her feet and Thomas caught her. He picked her up and was surprised by how light she was, as if his strong, proud grandmother had begun to hollow out without his noticing.

"Where is everyone?" Poppy asked.

"I expect they're in the drawing room," Thomas said. "It has all internal walls and the fireplace, so it's warm. Besides, I can put Mariette on the sofa there."

Mariette began to rally before they reached the drawing room. "Put me down, Thomas. There's no reason to make such a fuss."

"We're nearly there."

Mariette protested, but he ignored her, and when Poppy opened the doors to the study, he carried her in.

Arthur rushed to her side. "Is she all right? She refused to stay in here and demanded I remain and protect Miss Bethany."

"I'm fine," Mariette insisted. "Thomas is being melodramatic."

Thomas settled his angry grandmother on the sofa, and she immediately swung her feet to the floor and flapped her hands at him. "Leave me alone. I'm going to disown you for this."

"As long as you're all right, I'll manage," Thomas said, not particularly alarmed at his grandmother's threat. "How long ago did you reach the police?"

"Not long," Bethany said. "Right after we moved in here from the kitchen. I assume Mom told you about the call."

Thomas gaped at his mother in surprise. He wasn't sure when, if ever, she'd heard her call Mariette "Mom," but he was glad of the change in their relationship. Since they'd shared a room, he wondered if they'd stayed up having an honest heart-to-heart. He knew enough not to draw attention to it. "No details," he said. "She felt faint when we told her Mrs. Bing was dead."

"I'm right here," Mariette snapped. "Stop talking about me like I'm unconscious."

"Mrs. Bing is dead?" Cook wailed, then burst into tears. Thomas hadn't gotten the impression that Cook and Mrs. Bing were close, but he imagined everyone was nearing their breaking point.

"The police can't get here quick enough," Bethany said.

"I don't know about that," Cecil grumbled. "It's been my experience that the police rarely make matters better."

"Well, assuming they don't start stabbing anyone," Thomas said, "they'd be hard-pressed to make it worse."

"Since Thomas doesn't need Bethany's boat to summon the police," Cecil said, "I would like to use it. I would prefer to reach the village and my car as soon as possible so I can go home and put all this behind me."

"I don't think the police would appreciate that," Thomas said.

"I have virtually no interest whatsoever in what the police want," Cecil said.

"We do," Thomas replied firmly. "And I'm going to insist we stay right here, together, until the police arrive. I'm sure Arthur will help me enforce that, if necessary."

"Yes sir," Arthur agreed.

Cecil said nothing else, but he settled elegantly into one of the chairs near the fireplace where he radiated displeasure at everyone.

Thomas knelt by the sofa where Mariette sat. "Are you sure you're all right?"

"I'm fine. Stop hovering."

She did sound more or less normal, but Thomas couldn't get over how light she had been. He realized her clothes must have hidden some of her weight loss due to the illness that was slowly destroying her body. Still, he felt guilty for not seeing it.

Thomas stood and took a different chair, one close to the doors in case anyone decided to try to bolt. He specifically expected it of Cecil, but he had come to realize how full of surprises people were.

Poppy walked across the room and settled in a chair beside him. "Do you think the killer is outside somewhere?"

"I don't know," Thomas said. "He may be, though I'm concerned by how easily he is able to get in and out of the house. But for now, I think our best plan is simply waiting in a group for the police to arrive and handing the whole mess over to them."

"You're probably right." Facing the fireplace, Poppy tugged at the ends of her sleeves. "I became a ghostwriter because every job is different. I may have underestimated how different it could be."

"I suspect this is going to be the most extreme job you'll ever have," Thomas said.

Poppy huffed in what could have been a chuckle. "I do hope so."

Conversation was quiet and rare as the group waited for the police. Since the drawing room had no outside walls, the passing of time was hard to judge. There was a clock on the fireplace mantel, but it moved with unnatural slowness.

When the pounding finally came at the front door, everyone leaped to their feet, even Mariette. Relief washed over her face, and she stopped Arthur from moving toward the door. "This is my house. I will answer the door."

No one argued, and the grand woman sailed by Thomas. They all fell in line behind her. She flung open the front door and said, "Welcome to Winterhouse." There was no sign of hesitancy or frailty about her.

A man in his early sixties in a heavy wool coat stood outside, gazing at them steadily. "You called the police about a murder?"

"Several," Mariette said. "The count has gone up since my last call. I hope you brought help." Then her expression grew even sharper. "Do I know you? I believe I do."

"I hope you brought identification," Cecil spoke over Mariette. "As you can imagine, we're not eager to let unidentified strangers in, even if Mariette recognizes you vaguely."

The man reached into his coat pocket and produced an identification. "I'm Detective Mortenson. Bridger Mortenson."

"Bridger?" Bethany said, sudden delight in her voice. She'd been standing slightly to one side, but now edged in closer to the door. "Is that really you?"

The corners of the detective's mouth curled up, though his response couldn't be called anything as friendly as a smile. He inclined his head. "Bethany. It's been a long time."

"That's where I know you from." Mariette's face suggested she'd tasted something sour. "You're the police officer who dated Bethany for a while."

"It's been a few years," the detective said. "May I come in? I need to examine the bodies. I also need to know how many murders we're talking about."

"Three bodies," Thomas said. "But they may not all be murders. Some may have been accidents, though I'm disinclined to believe it since the housekeeper was stabbed."

Detective Mortenson blinked at him. "Then I'd better see them. Are they inside?"

"This way," Mariette said, taking up the hostess role.

"One moment." The detective used his two-way radio to contact what Thomas assumed were the other officers who'd arrived on the island with him, telling them to come to the house and to bring the coroner. "Can someone let them in when they arrive?"

"I will," Arthur offered.

"And you are?"

"Arthur Kent here is my butler," Mariette said.

"You'll need this, sir." Arthur held out a single key. "It's to the lock on the conservatory. Mr. Nordwich thought it best we keep the room locked to protect the evidence."

"Mr. Nordwich?"

Thomas introduced himself.

"Thank you for keeping the room with the bodies locked." Mortenson studied his face. "You're Bethany's son?"

"I am."

The man took the key without further comment, then shifted his attention to the larger group. "And the rest of you?"

Introductions were quick, with the detective offering almost no commentary.

Once they were done, the detective indicated that he was ready to see the bodies. The entire group, other than Arthur, followed Mariette and Detective Mortenson through the house to the conservatory.

"Did you come on the ferry?" Mariette asked as they strolled through the halls.

"No," Mortenson said. "Neither Cass nor his boat could be found this morning. Considering the blizzard, we've alerted the coast guard."

"You think he was out in the storm?" Mariette asked.

"I don't know," Mortenson replied, his formal tone finally falling away. "When Cass is sober, he's as sensible about the water as anyone you'll find. But I've no way of knowing what his condition was. He's paid more than one fine for being out on the boat when he wasn't fit to sail."

They reached the doors to the conservatory. Mortenson paused to don latex gloves from his coat pocket. "Who has been in this room?"

"I have," Poppy said. "I was trying to find Jacqueline when she didn't show up to breakfast. She wasn't in her room, so I went room to room until I found her in the conservatory. I took her pulse and realized she was dead."

"Has anyone else been in there?"

"I went in," Mariette said. "Jacqueline was my friend, and I wanted to know what happened to her. I insisted we make some kind of cursory examination, and Poppy realized the woman's skull was damaged under that ridiculous wig she always wore."

"Anyone else?"

"Me," Thomas said. "And Arthur. We carried Teddy Marcone in here after he collapsed and died in the drawing room. And Arthur covered the bodies. He didn't think it was proper to simply leave them."

"You said there were three bodies," the detective said. "Where is the third?"

"Outside where I found it," Thomas said. "The housekeeper, Mrs. Elizabeth Bing, disappeared yesterday. Poppy and I went out searching for her this morning. We found her near the family boathouse. She'd been stabbed. We left her where she was, and I didn't get close enough to touch the body."

"That's something, at least." He gazed at Cook. "Have you been in this room?"

"No sir," Cook said. "I'm the cook. I had no reason to come in here, and I didn't."

"And you?" the detective asked Cecil.

"No," the elegant man said coolly.

"That's something, anyway. All of you wait out here. When the coroner arrives, please make way for him and the rest of my officers."

And with that, Mortenson unlocked the door, pulled the chain from around the handles, and let himself in.

When the door closed behind Mortenson, Thomas took a step closer to his mother. "You dated him?"

"It was a long time ago, but yes. I liked him. Your grandparents didn't. They thought he was 'unacceptable,'" Bethany said the last word in her snootiest tone.

"He was," Mariette said. "You were too good to marry a policeman."

Bethany didn't argue, but Thomas could practically see unspoken words hanging in the air between them. They'd gained some ground in their relationship, and he wondered if they were trying to guard that by not arguing further about Mortenson.

Finally Bethany wasn't able to restrain herself. She told Thomas, "You'll find there weren't many people in the village that my parents didn't manage to upset or alienate in some way through the years."

"We had no desire to mix with people from the village," Mariette said. "But we employed people. We weren't impolite."

"I'm not sure you know what 'impolite' means," Bethany said.

"I don't know about that," Mariette said. "I can hear how impolite you're being."

So much for the end of the arguing.

"Excuse us, please," a voice called behind the group.

Everyone moved closer to the walls. Well, nearly everyone. Cecil refused to step aside and allow easier passage for the two new people who'd arrived. One of the newcomers was a uniformed police officer. He was younger than Thomas and wore his trim uniform under a thick parka that had police insignia sewn into it.

The second man who followed behind the officer, carrying a large bag slung over one shoulder, was considerably older. Thomas would guess his age at no less than seventy. He had pale white eyebrows and equally pale gray eyes. His neatly styled hair was white at the temples and salt-and-pepper near the back. He had fine wrinkles and deep crow's feet, suggesting he'd spent considerable time outside. Thomas guessed he was the coroner.

The conservatory door opened, and the detective stepped out. "Dr. Vine," he said, confirming Thomas's guess. "There are two bodies inside and allegedly a third outside."

"Give me a bit to examine these two, and then I'll go outside," Dr. Vine said.

"That should be fine," Mortenson said. He shifted his attention to the officer again. "And you can lead these people to a single room where you can watch over them."

"The drawing room would work," Thomas said. "There's a fire. We were in there when you arrived."

"Good idea," Mortenson said. "But I'll need you to show me to the third body. I want to see it. I assume you remember the way."

"Of course." But something about the way Mortenson's suspicious eyes bored into him made Thomas wonder if the fact that he'd found the body wasn't sitting well with the detective. *Terrific.*

"I was with Thomas," Poppy said. "Outside, when he found the body."

"Okay," Mortenson said. "You can come with us to show me the body. I may have some questions along the way."

Poppy wasn't excited about drawing the man's attention to her, but she hadn't liked the way he'd been sizing up Thomas. Mortenson had just arrived and knew virtually nothing about what was going on. Once he did, he'd surely direct his suspicious gaze somewhere else. In the meanwhile, she was happy to do what she could to get them through it.

As they stepped out in the cold, Mortenson began to question Thomas. "Was Mrs. Winter having some kind of party?"

"A weekend gathering," Thomas explained. "My grandmother intends to write her memoirs. That's why Poppy is here. She's a ghostwriter. Since the memoir will affect a number of her old friends, Mariette invited them to Winterhouse to let them know."

"Old friends would include the two deceased in the conservatory?" Mortenson guessed. "And Cecil Lewis, I assume."

"That's right," Thomas confirmed.

They reached a treacherous part of the path, and the conversation halted while they made their way carefully to avoid a fall. Poppy noticed the snow was melting in the spots where the sun could reach the path. That made the walking messier, but not as slippery.

When they were on more solid ground, Mortenson resumed his questioning. "How did Mrs. Winter's old friends react to the news of the memoir?"

"They were surprised and unhappy," Thomas said. "Mariette announced the news over dinner on Friday night. Cecil, Teddy, and Jacqueline intended to leave Saturday morning in protest of Mariette's plan."

"But they didn't," Mortenson said.

"The storm prevented Cecil and Teddy's exit," Thomas said. His voice was so calm that he could be reciting a book he'd read. Poppy wasn't sure his completely detached recitation was making Mortenson any less suspicious. "Then Poppy discovered Jacqueline, and Cecil left the house to go to the boathouse. He planned to take the family boat to the village."

"That wasn't a good idea in a blizzard," Mortenson said.

"No, but it didn't happen either. I went down to the boathouse to speak with Cecil and convince him not to leave in the storm, and he showed me that the boat had been sabotaged. Someone had put a hole in it."

"I see. And Mr. Marcone's death?"

"He died Saturday night after supper," Thomas said. "He apparently had some sort of medical condition. But after Mrs. Bing vanished, Poppy and I checked her quarters and found an aconite plant."

"I don't know what that is," Mortenson said.

"It's wolfsbane," Poppy said.

"The plant from the old horror movies? How is that relevant?"

"It's extremely poisonous," Thomas said, "and the symptoms of interacting with it or ingesting it mirror a heart attack."

"How do you know that?" Mortenson asked.

"Research for a book I wrote."

The detective's gaze shifted from Poppy to Thomas. "You're both writers."

"I'm a ghostwriter," Poppy said. "Thomas is a college professor who wrote a book."

Thomas raised an eyebrow at her, obviously wondering why she'd clarified in that way. She wasn't sure why either. Maybe she was being helpful. Maybe she was still stung by reference to the book that had caused so much trouble years before.

"I see." Mortenson asked more questions as they walked, and seemed acutely interested when he learned about the hidden room and the intruder who had been in the attic. "And you have no idea of the person's identity."

"I'm afraid not," Thomas said. "Beyond the fact that it wasn't Mrs. Bing. It was a man."

When they reached the steep area where Mrs. Bing's body waited, the detective accepted Thomas's assistance in getting down close to the spot. Poppy hated being left behind on the path, but she didn't want to upset the detective any further.

"You didn't put these branches over her?" the detective asked.

"No," Thomas said. "I didn't go that close."

"Hello?" a voice called. The coroner was picking his way carefully down the path with Arthur's assistance. "You should have waited for me."

"I haven't touched the body," Mortenson assured him. "You finished with the other two quickly."

"I'm not finished," the coroner said. "But I didn't want anyone muddying up this crime scene."

"I wanted to see the setting," Mortenson said, taking no apparent offense at Dr. Vine's tone. "You'll need help getting down."

Thomas scrambled up the hill, and between him and Arthur, they helped the coroner reach the spot where Mrs. Bing was half hidden.

"You knew her?" Thomas asked when Dr. Vine's posture stiffened at the sight of the body. "You seem upset."

"I knew her slightly," the coroner said. "I'd met her, which always makes this sort of thing harder. She worked for some people I knew. She always struck me as a good person."

"I thought so too," Thomas said.

Dr. Vine relaxed slightly. "I'm glad you agree."

"Will this be a problem for the work?" Detective Mortenson asked. "We need someone who can be objective."

"I will be fine. Besides, I'm the only coroner you have here. If you have to wait on someone else, it will be some time."

"Sure, but I don't want anything to mess up this investigation," the detective said. "Especially when it's clear this lady was murdered."

"Yes," Dr. Vine agreed. "That much is clear."

"We'll leave you to it, then. Come along, Mr. Nordwich, Mr. Kent." Mortenson climbed up to the path where Poppy waited. "No one has any idea what brought the victim outside?"

"No," Poppy said. "In fact, I would have thought she'd be afraid to go much of anywhere alone. I actually wondered if the intruder forced her outside, but I can't imagine why. And you can see she has on her outerwear. I have a hard time believing a kidnapper would pause to let her put that on."

"When was the last time anyone saw her?" Mortenson asked.

Poppy explained how Mrs. Bing had been with her on the stairs of the lighthouse tower but had not wanted to continue. "She said she was going to the kitchen so Cook wouldn't be alone. We were trying not to wander around alone. The blizzard and the deaths had everyone on edge. At any rate, she never made it to the kitchen."

"How do you know that?"

"Cook said she hadn't seen her," Poppy answered. "No one else had either—not after she left me in the tower."

"So you were the last to see Mrs. Bing alive," Mortenson said.

"But we know exactly where Poppy was," Thomas said as he finished the climb to join them. "She was with my mother in the tower room."

"I wasn't accusing anyone," the detective replied mildly.

"It's obvious that the intruder who'd been hiding in the secret room was also the one who has been killing people," Thomas said.

"An intruder that no one but you and Miss Hayes saw," Mortenson said.

"Everyone saw the man's things in the secret room."

"Of course." But Mortenson continued to radiate distrust, if not disdain. "And I will, of course, want to examine and collect fingerprints from the secret room. How many of you paraded through it in the search for this intruder?"

"I don't appreciate your tone, Detective," Thomas said.

"I'm sorry," Mortenson said, and it almost sounded sincere. "Being suspicious comes with the job, I suppose. But I'd be lying if I said it isn't awfully convenient for a mysterious intruder to be the killer. It takes the pressure off everyone else."

"I recognize that you're trying to do your job," Thomas said, his voice tight with the strain of staying calm and professional. "But baseless accusations won't help anyone, and can in fact do irreparable damage."

"I'll be questioning everyone, because everyone here is a potential suspect," Mortenson said. "I'd be derelict in my duties if I did not approach this objectively."

"Do you have any theories about why Thomas or I would kill anyone here?" Poppy asked. "Every single person here, with the exception of Mariette Winter, was a perfect stranger to me before this weekend, and I'd only talked to Mariette on the phone." She decided not to mention her unfortunate first meeting with Thomas.

"Your motive, I assume," Mortenson said, "would be protecting your boyfriend."

Poppy felt her face flush. "No one here is my boyfriend."

"Of course not." Mortenson called down to the coroner. "Dr. Vine, if you're good here, I'm going up to the house and check out this secret room I've been told about."

"I'm good," the coroner called out. "I'll keep the butler, if that's okay. I may need a hand up."

"That should be fine. I'll send an officer to replace him."

Mortenson, Thomas, and Poppy headed to the house. The path was easier to navigate uphill toward the house than it had been going down, so they made better time. As Poppy trudged through the snow and the slush, she remembered thinking that everything would get better once the police arrived. Apparently she'd been wrong. They may not be in danger of being murdered, but they were in for some uncomfortable hours, especially if Mortenson didn't even believe there was an intruder on the island.

Would he even try to find the real killer? Poppy cut her eyes to the side to watch the detective. She hadn't enjoyed his insinuation, but he still could be good at his job. He'd been thrown into the deep end with the case. But it was essential that the police find the intruder. With the blizzard over, the intruder could get off the island. If he did that, would the police stand any chance of catching him?

And would that make Thomas the best available suspect? He'd be the lone man under seventy years old, and that alone worried her. Deeply.

16

$\mathcal{F}$or the first time, walking into the house didn't come with an immediate sense of relief. Poppy was glad to be out of the cold, but the weather was the least of their problems at the moment. As soon as they reached the house, the police detective stopped to answer his phone. Apparently more boats had arrived, and the detective quickly gave orders for collecting evidence.

Poppy was pleased to see that Mortenson did set a couple of officers to the task of searching the island for any other people. He might not believe Poppy and Thomas's story about the intruder, but he was a good enough detective to leave no stone unturned. Hopefully they'd find something to set the investigation on the right track.

"I need to speak to your grandmother," Mortenson said when he finished the call.

"She's probably in the drawing room with the others," Thomas said. "It's this way."

They found the group waiting more or less patiently. Cecil glared at everyone around him. Cook twisted her fingers together nervously. Mariette and Bethany sat close together on one of the sofas. Seeing their matching expressions of strained patience cheered Poppy. As awful as everything was, she was glad to see mother and daughter mending their relationship.

"Mrs. Winter," Mortenson said, "I need to speak to each of you alone. It's a few routine questions, but I prefer to hear each person speak without the influence of the others. Is there a room that would be conducive to this?"

"There is a sitting room on this floor that I use as an office of sorts," Mariette said. "It's smaller than this room, so I imagine it will be good for your purposes. May I assume we are all suspects?"

"You are all sources of vital information to the case," Mortenson replied diplomatically.

Mariette laughed. "Well, I shall imagine that I am a suspect, as it amuses me. Since I'm eighty-five, not many people consider me capable of the kind of athleticism required to drag young women out into a storm."

"I try not to underestimate anyone," Mortenson said.

"Will we wait in here to be summoned to the questioning?"

"No," the detective said. "I have techs coming. They will arrive in the next few minutes. They will need to examine this room because I've been told Teddy Marcone died here, and I understand it might not have been natural causes."

Mariette sighed. "I prefer to think it was natural. No one died in the dining room. Shall we wait there?"

"That sounds agreeable."

"Detective," Thomas said. "I retained the glass Teddy drank whiskey from before he died. It's up in my room. Shall I retrieve it?"

"No," Mortenson said. "Techs will be going over all your rooms. I will make sure they watch for the glass and collect it. Why did you keep the glass when everyone believed he died of natural causes?"

"I found it too coincidental so close after Jacqueline's death."

"Thomas has a suspicious nature that you'll probably find much like your own, Detective," Mariette said. "Would you consider interviewing me first? To be honest, I'm rather tired, and you may want to ask your questions while I have the energy to answer them."

Poppy felt a thrill of alarm. It wasn't like Mariette to admit to weakness of any kind.

"Are you all right?" Thomas asked his grandmother, concern showing on his features.

"I'm fine. Don't fuss. I merely said I was tired. Last night—this whole weekend, really—was rather harrowing for all of us."

"I am happy to begin with you, Mrs. Winter," Mortenson cut in.

So the group relocated to the dining room.

"Would anyone like coffee?" Cook asked, obviously desperate for a distraction.

"I would prefer that everyone sit and wait until I finish this questioning," Mortenson told her.

Without another word, Cook sat down stiffly on a chair near the window.

When the detective escorted Mariette out of the room, the police officer who had waited with the group in the drawing room took up his station next to the door, effectively a guard to ensure they stayed in place.

Poppy nudged Thomas, then took a seat as far from the police officer as possible, sitting in the chair that was normally reserved for Mariette. Thomas followed to take the chair next to hers. "I'm concerned," Poppy said quietly. "I get the impression the detective doesn't believe the intruder exists."

"I believe you're correct," Thomas said, "but he did send people out to search. That makes me feel better about him. I hope it's merely his professional integrity to keep an open mind. Now that there are people actively collecting evidence and prints, I'm sure the detective will lose interest in me as a suspect."

Poppy wasn't sure she agreed. If the police actually found the intruder, that would confirm it. But the man had proved surprisingly elusive.

How many times had they searched for him without success? And if Thomas, who knew the house well, couldn't find the intruder, who could?

Bethany got up from her chair and came to sit on Poppy's other side. "What are you two up to?"

"The detective thinks Thomas is the killer," Poppy said angrily. "He didn't believe us about the intruder. We need to be outside finding the real murderer. Thomas knows the island better than the officers."

"We can't join the search," Thomas said. "I'm certain the police officer at the door would object."

Bethany grinned. "That really shouldn't be a problem. He's not paying attention to us. Haven't you noticed? He's facing the end of the hall, probably looking out the windows around the front door. He's young, and he's itching for real duty."

"I don't see how that makes anything easier," Thomas said. "He would hardly miss it if we walk by him."

"You're being silly, darling," his mother said. "After all, there's a door right there." She tipped her head toward the second door leading from the dining room and into the hallway to the kitchen. It was made in the traditional manner of doors designed for use by servants and matched the paneled wall perfectly. Poppy had seen Mrs. Bing and Arthur go in and out that door, so it hadn't been hard for her to spot the outline. But the police officer had not. "He doesn't know about the second door. He's not keeping an eye on us. You guys could leave and join the search if you wanted."

"I don't know," Thomas said. "I don't see how that could make us be judged less guilty."

Bethany groaned. "Finding the intruder will prove you aren't guilty."

"I would rather trust the system," Thomas said.

Bethany huffed and settled in her chair.

Poppy watched the young police officer. For the most part, he did appear uninterested in them, though when Cecil got up and began pacing, it drew the officer's attention instantly. The young man surveyed the room, his gaze touching on each of them before he said, "It shouldn't be too much longer."

Cecil snapped, "I don't believe that for a second." Then he dropped into a chair and glared out one of the tall dining room windows.

Once the young officer was facing down the hall again, Poppy said quietly, "Movement in here draws his attention. I don't think we could get out the kitchen door if we wanted to."

Bethany studied the police officer. "Maybe."

Finally Detective Mortenson returned with Mariette and called for Cecil. The older man stomped out in a huff.

Bethany whispered to Poppy and Thomas. "Wait for your opportunity."

"What?" Thomas asked, but his mother didn't reply.

Instead, she stood and crossed the room to put an arm around her mother. Mariette startled, staring at her daughter in clear surprise but didn't resist as Bethany led her to a chair, murmuring to her.

Once the detective and Cecil were gone and the officer had resumed staring down the hall, Mariette rose from the chair where she'd been whispering with Bethany and strode to the young officer. As he turned to face her, everything about Mariette's posture drooped, and the elderly woman suddenly looked frail and shaky.

Mariette spoke quietly to the officer, ignoring his obvious attempts to get her to go into the room and sit. Mariette kept talking quietly while fluttering her hands. The officer put a hand on Mariette's arm as if to placate her. The older woman suddenly gasped and grabbed at her chest.

Bethany leaped from her chair and raced to Mariette's side. "What did you do to my mother?" she shrieked.

Bethany put her arm around Mariette, maneuvering her gently so she was directing the officer's attention away from Poppy and Thomas, who'd stood when Mariette had appeared to take ill. The young officer stammered out a protest that he hadn't done anything as Bethany continued to berate him.

Thomas and Poppy exchanged a glance. It was now or never. As one, they moved smoothly over to the other door, slipped through, and ran for the kitchen and the outside door there. They would find the killer and clear Thomas's name.

Certain that he could not have made a worse decision, Thomas led Poppy around the rear of the house and into a small patch of trees. They hadn't been able to find proper coats to go out in that kind of weather, not without risking the attention of the officers. One rather worn raincoat had hung from a peg near the door in the mudroom, and Thomas had insisted Poppy wear it. She'd wrinkled her nose at the musty smell coming off it but had not resisted. The sleeves covered her hands in a way he found endearing.

The temperature had continued to rise, though it was still much too cold for the sweater Thomas wore. He hoped walking would help, so he tried to pick up the pace as he held Poppy by the hand. It was the first time he'd held her hand without gloves between then, and he found he enjoyed it.

They had a nervous moment when they had to crouch behind some brush to hide from an officer leading Arthur to the house. The officer never looked in their direction, which was good. Their hiding place was not as secure as Thomas hoped, since Arthur glanced their way once and tipped his head slightly.

Once Arthur and the officer were gone, Thomas and Poppy began moving again.

"Where are we going?" Poppy whispered.

"We can reach the cove this way. It's rougher, but I think we're less likely to be seen if we go through the trees rather than along the path."

"Maybe the intruder thought that too," Poppy said, a slight tremble in her voice.

It was possible. They had circled the house on previous searches, but then they'd gone down the usual path. The killer could have avoided them by staying off the paths. Thomas also knew that without the path, the downhill slope would eventually become challenging.

"Why do we want your mother's boat?"

"I think that cove must be where the killer has a boat," Thomas said. "There aren't that many places to tie up on the island. There are no beaches, but there are plenty of cliffs. They're not huge, but they are too steep to climb up from the water, and the water below them is lousy with rocks that could be super dangerous in a fall."

They moved through the trees as quietly as possible. Thomas was grateful for the muted colors he wore. The drab, dark-green raincoat covered most of Poppy's outfit. Perhaps that would help them avoid being seen by any police out searching.

Poppy froze suddenly, tugging hard on Thomas's arm, and he gave her a questioning glance. She mouthed, "Voices."

He stood still, trying to quiet his breathing and listen. He did hear the faint sound of voices. It was probably the police officers, whom he and Poppy should elude, but something made Thomas want to be sure. *Won't be the stupidest decision I've made lately.* He jerked his head in the direction of the sound and began creeping toward it.

Eventually they drew close enough that Thomas recognized one of the voices. It was the coroner. Thomas turned to face Poppy to pass that along and saw shock on her face. "What?" he asked softly.

She waved him down close to her and leaned close to him. She whispered in his ear, her breath tickling his skin. "That's the coroner and Cass Andrews."

"I thought they couldn't find Cass," Thomas murmured.

"Guess he showed up." She jerked her thumb in a different direction, her suggestion clear—that they should avoid the speakers.

But Thomas found he really wanted to hear what the two men were talking about, so he shook his head. Though something in her face suggested she didn't approve of his plan, Poppy didn't resist, and they crept closer. Up ahead, a tall rock jutted out of the landscape, a common feature in New England.

They hugged the rock closely, appreciating the cover, and edged slowly around it to hear better. Finally they could see the two men standing on another jutting rock, almost level with the ground. Thomas knew that rock. He had sometimes daydreamed while sitting on it when he visited his grandmother, imagining daring adventures and thrilling heroics. It stuck out over the highest cliff on the island. Below lurked rough water and a cluster of sharp rocks. The sense of danger was one of the things he'd loved about the spot as a boy.

With both men visible, their voices were clearer too. Thomas crouched, feeling Poppy kneel beside him. The body language between the two men on the rock set off red flags in his mind. They huddled together, furtive and angry.

"You've messed this up about as far as humanly possible," the coroner snapped, looming over the shorter, thicker ferry captain.

Cass took a reluctant step closer to the edge of the rock. "I had to improvise."

"You killed the wrong person," Dr. Vine complained. "Twice.

And you were seen. I have to assume you were drunk this whole time, which astounds me."

"I was not," Cass growled. "I haven't touched a drop. And don't get all high and mighty with me. You'd have been confused too. That actress was the spitting image of Mariette Winter when she was swanning around in the dark. I didn't want to miss a chance to take out the old witch when she'd practically fallen into my lap."

"Which doesn't lessen the damage done by being seen."

"It's not my fault the old woman's daughter remembered her secret room and sent everyone hunting for me. I hadn't counted on Bethany being here at all. Your 'inside man' wasn't so useful there. But no one will guess it was me. I covered my face when I was caught in the attic."

The coroner groaned, apparently disgusted with the man. "And the housekeeper?" he asked. "Did you somehow confuse her with Cecil Lewis, you bumbling idiot?" Again Dr. Vine stepped toward Cass, and again the ferry captain retreated, though not more than a small step.

Cass narrowed his eyes. "I won't be talked to that way. That housekeeper was falling apart. You never should have brought her into this. Apparently she wasn't as indebted to you as you thought, because she was going to crack and spill everything. I didn't have any choice. Killing her *saved* the plan—it didn't ruin it."

"So says you," Dr. Vine said. "She's not here to defend herself. The girl was desperate for money, and I paid her well. And since Teddy is dead, I'm assuming she did her part. Unless you're going to claim you poisoned him."

"No. I'd have knocked him over the head, same as the actress. Poison is too unpredictable, and I told her as much. What if he hadn't drunk the whiskey? Or what if someone had joined him? Then we'd have more bodies you didn't want. But she said Teddy told her he drank a glass of whiskey every night after dinner and slept like a lamb because of it. So she poisoned the bottle in his room in addition to the whiskey glasses. It was all too complicated."

"Her plan is the one that actually worked."

"Hardly," Cass sneered. "The housekeeper said she expected the plant you gave her to make Teddy sick, nothing more. Apparently you told her it wouldn't be fatal. She swore she didn't want to kill anyone. The guilt was making a mess of the woman."

"Her not knowing was part of the plan," the coroner said. "That way she couldn't turn informant, or she'd be admitting to murder."

"Your brilliant plan wasn't working, I tell you. She was ready to blab everything to anyone who would listen. Besides, it makes no sense to discuss things that have already happened. What you have to do now is help get me off this island. My boat is in a cove." He pointed off in the direction Thomas had been planning to go. He'd been right about the intruder's escape plan. "All you have to do is make sure there's no cops in the way so I can leave."

"You were supposed to be off the island before the storm ended."

"The job wasn't done. Are you saying you'd have paid full price with one of the three targets gone?"

"You'll be lucky if I pay you anything," Dr. Vine snarled. "And I won't do anything to draw suspicion toward me. I'll do what I can with the postmortems, and make sure there's no evidence of your involvement there, but that's all I can do. I can't protect you with the hash you've made of the plan."

"I can come back later. Right now there is no way for me to reach Cecil or Mariette, but they'll let their guard down eventually. All you have to do is keep my name out of it and we can still finish the job." Cass poked Dr. Vine's coat with one rough finger. "If I'm caught, I'll drag you down with me. After all, I'm not the one who killed Matthew Bellamy. You made that mess, and once they know that, I'm sure they'll find the evidence easily enough. But if I get away, you can pin the murders on Cecil Lewis. Anyone would believe he could kill people. And think about it—having a rich guy go to prison for what's left of his life will be justice enough."

"Have you lost your mind?" Dr. Vine hissed. "That'll never work."

"Sure it will. The housekeeper said Mariette is really sick. She's dying. You don't have to do anything to her. Send Cecil to jail, and it will be happy endings all around."

Dr. Vine considered it in silence, then finally said, "I'll keep that in mind. But it doesn't change the fact that you're a loose end I can't risk."

And to Thomas's shock, the coroner lunged toward the ferry captain, his hands raised into fists.

Cass jumped at the display of aggression, but there wasn't room for that jump. He'd hit the edge. He grabbed for Dr. Vine, but the older man merely slapped his hand away.

Cass plummeted over the side of the rock.

For an instant, Poppy couldn't believe what she'd seen. She waited for Cass to scramble up the rock, but he didn't. What should they do? She was so shocked that she barely noticed when Dr. Vine walked toward them, pulling a gun from inside his coat and aiming it in their direction.

"Come on out," he said. "Don't think you can outrun a bullet."

Thomas stepped forward, taking Poppy's hand but keeping her behind him. She was touched by his protective streak but strongly hoped neither of them were about to be shot.

"Since this is your family's island, I assume you can make a good guess as to where Cass would have hidden his ferry," Dr. Vine said, as if it were any other day and he were having any other conversation, rather than holding a gun on two people after ensuring that another fell off a cliff.

"I'm fairly sure, but why do you need his ferry?" Thomas asked, matching his conversational tone. "Can't you leave in the boat you came in?"

"Oh, the ferry isn't for me," Dr. Vine said with an almost indulgent smile. "It's for you. Mortenson is already suspicious of you two. You two are going to make a run for it and go down in history as a local Bonnie and Clyde. Isn't that exciting? Unfortunately, that old tub of Cass's is an accident waiting to happen. A fiery accident, actually." He shook his head, tsking.

"I don't suppose you'd change your mind if we promised not to tell anyone about your being the mastermind of the murders," Poppy said.

"I don't suppose so," the coroner agreed. "Let's go." He waved the barrel of the pistol in the direction they'd been planning to go earlier.

"This plan sounds tidy," Poppy said, not immediately moving. "But I don't think it's going to hold up. I don't believe that police detective is as stupid as you think."

"He's not stupid at all," the older man said. "But he has considerable lingering resentment toward the Winters. Apparently they hurt his pride when he was a young man." He waved the gun again, adding. "Don't make me shoot you both. I can find a way to make it fit my scenario, but I hate making a mess."

"Pushing a man off a cliff isn't messy?" Thomas asked.

Dr. Vine smirked. "I'm barely rumpled. Now move."

They moved. Poppy sensed that the man enjoyed the sound of his own voice, and they already knew it carried well. Maybe if they got him talking, someone else would hear him. "How does a coroner become a murderer anyway?"

"It's not exactly something I wanted," Dr. Vine said.

"And yet, here we are," Thomas replied.

"Shut up," the older man growled. "You don't know anything. It was Joseph Winter who brought us to where we are."

"How did my grandfather do that?" Thomas demanded, and Poppy winced. They wanted the coroner talking, but too much provoking could be fatal.

"I was the doctor hired by Joseph Winter to certify that none of the people who came into contact with a certain toxic pesticide had suffered any ill effects. I examined dying men, women, and children and came up with an alternate diagnosis every time—something that allowed the Winter lawyer to pay them off and keep the company name clean."

"And were you forced into this job?"

"Hardly. I was paid extremely well. Well enough that I've lived a contented life ever since."

"But not guilt free," Poppy suggested.

"I don't feel guilty for what I did. It's the way of the world. The strong build their empires upon the weak. No, I don't have a problem with what I did, but I am well aware that others would. I'm not a young man, but I have no interest in spending the rest of my life as a social pariah."

"Better to spend it in prison?" Thomas asked.

"That will never happen."

"That still doesn't explain why you wanted to kill Matthew, Teddy, Cecil, and Mariette," Poppy said.

"I thought you were a bright girl," the coroner said. "It's that wretched book, of course. The one you were hired to come here and write, which would expose the dirty deeds of the Winter businesses."

"Why would Mariette do that?" Poppy said, though she already knew. Mariette had brought up the pesticide problem at their meeting.

"Guilt? Piety? I don't know why, and I don't care. I only know that it was going to happen. Matthew Bellamy called me to tell me that I would probably want to leave the country, perhaps go to some quiet place that didn't extradite criminals to the US. He said he was going to use the memoir to come clean about everything he'd been part of. He was ready to face the music. I was not."

"So you went to his home and killed him," Poppy said.

"I did," the coroner said. "First, I tried to get him to tell me how much Mariette knew. He said she didn't know anything that would implicate me, but I suspected he was lying. He was kind enough to let me know about this convenient little weekend gathering where all the people who could possibly cause a problem for me would be in one place."

"And you decided to kill them," Thomas said.

"Not me personally," Dr. Vine corrected him. "I made sure I had plenty of alibis, especially in light of my more hands-on approach with Matthew. I hired Cass Andrews. He was in dire financial straits. He'd borrowed money from some bad people to keep his fishing business going. And he would do anything to pay the debt he owed."

"And Mrs. Bing?" Poppy said.

"I knew her as well. She also needed money—not as badly, but bad enough. She'd stolen money from her last employer and gotten fired. Because of why she was fired, she was having a hard time finding new work. I arranged some false references and paid her. Not as much as I promised Cass, but I'm sure it sounded like a fortune to someone in her situation."

"But she didn't agree to murder," Poppy said.

"She would have been fine," Dr. Vine growled. "That idiot fisherman made a mess of everything." His voice sharpened when he said, "We're off the path."

"We have to be," Thomas said. "The cove isn't normally used so there's no direct path. That's why it's a good place to hide."

"You better not be trying to trick me," the older man said.

Poppy tripped on a snow-slick rock, and Thomas grabbed her hand to keep her from falling—or at least that's what she thought. But instead of simply steadying her, he whispered urgently, "Jump."

She hadn't realized how close they were to the edge of the cliff until Thomas tugged on her arm, pulling her between two trees that leaned away as if they were peering over the edge of the cliff. Then Thomas put an arm around her and jumped, dragging her along with him.

Poppy screamed so loud she barely heard the coroner bellowing after them. He was the least of her worries as the raging surf rushed up to meet her.

The second they hit the icy water, Thomas felt Poppy jerked away from him by the force of the impact. The cliff was far lower than the one where the coroner had pushed Cass Andrews, but it was still high enough to make them hit hard.

Dazed, he flailed around searching for Poppy. He didn't find her, and water closed over his head, pushing him down and down. The cold was beyond anything he'd ever experienced. It cut through the shock of impact, but he knew that it would also sap his strength quickly. For the first time he was grateful for the fact that he hadn't been able to grab his coat, so that he could push off from the bottom and swim hard for the surface without the drag of heavy, sodden fabric.

The water was dark as he rose, and he still didn't see Poppy. Was she all right? He thought of the raincoat she wore. Would it be enough to drag her down? By trying to save them, had he actually ensured that Poppy would drown?

He'd known the spot where they'd jumped was directly above the opening to the cove where his mother had left her boat, the cove that had been their eventual destination. The water deepened there in a quirk of current, time, and geology, but it was the one spot where rocks didn't threaten anyone falling. That was why they often swam there. It was the deepest water around the island.

Thomas finally broke the surface and searched frantically for Poppy. She had to be here. She couldn't have drowned. He considered diving to find her, but the water was too dark. He'd never find her that way.

Then Poppy's head popped up at a spot farther into the cove. He would have cheered if he'd had the energy. The current was carrying him that way as well. He began to swim toward her. The cold robbed him of the ease he normally felt in the water, having been a swimmer all his life, but he wouldn't let it keep him from reaching Poppy.

Any swimmer in such cold had scant minutes before the cold drained them so completely that drowning would be in a race with hypothermia for which could kill first. With her smaller size, the cold would take Poppy sooner than him if they didn't get out of the water.

Poppy swam for the nearest rock, doing better than he'd expected, though he could already see her strokes were slowing. He caught up with her and looped an arm around her middle. Together they managed the last yards to the rock.

Thomas pushed her up onto the rock before scrambling up himself. Poppy lay on her side, gasping and trembling, but Thomas couldn't let her rest. They weren't out of danger yet. They hadn't drowned, but hypothermia was a serious problem. He scrambled over to Poppy and tugged on her arm. "We have to get to the ferry," he said through his own gasps. "The cold will kill us here."

Poppy rolled onto her stomach to scramble to her feet. She wasn't fast, but she was still moving, and he was proud of her. He stood on leaden legs, but he put his arm around Poppy and helped her over the rocks toward the ferry. A smaller boat was tied up near it. He considered taking his mother's boat but knew they were more likely to find something to wrap up in aboard the larger craft.

By the time they reached the old fishing boat that served as the Winterhouse ferry, Thomas and Poppy were staggering. The jump from the closest rock to the deck of the boat was too much for Poppy, so Thomas practically tossed her over. She landed in a heap on the deck but didn't complain. Thomas was concerned by how quiet Poppy had gotten. He needed to help her get warm.

He jumped onto the deck and his legs gave out under him, but he soon stood again, though each movement was made by sheer strength of will. "Come on, Poppy." He dragged her into the cabin and began opening every cupboard or storage area. He found several grubby sweatshirts crammed in a box alongside some towels. They weren't ideal, but they would be better than nothing. He shook Poppy. "Can you change yourself, or do you need my help?"

She rallied. "I can change myself," she said through chattering teeth.

The teeth chattering and shivers were actually a good sign. The worst hypothermia came after the shivering stopped.

He grabbed a sweater from the box. "Put on all the rest," he said, then stepped out of the wheelhouse, peeling off his wet sweater and pulling on the dry one. It smelled of fish, but Thomas was grateful for the fresh warmth. Too bad the man didn't have a stash of dry jeans.

"Are you done?" he called.

"D-done," Poppy stammered.

Thomas stepped into the wheelhouse and started the boat engine. He knew the sound was sure to draw Dr. Vine, but they needed to get away. They could circle to the main dock and tie up near the police boats. Surely there would be an officer there who could help them.

"I need to cast off," Thomas said to Poppy, who huddled near the heater.

"I can do that," Poppy said, standing. Her lips still had a blue cast, but her voice was stronger. Thomas hated to let her go out in the cold, but he felt he'd dragged her around enough. She wouldn't thank him for treating her as a burden.

"Thanks," he said.

Once they were free, Thomas steered the boat away from the rocks and out of the cove. The second they hit open water, shots rang out. The coroner had found them.

"Poppy!" Thomas shouted, cursing himself for letting her out of the wheelhouse.

She stumbled in, hugging herself. "I'm fine."

"No, you're not," Thomas yelled. He could see blood on the sleeve of the sweatshirt.

"I'm good," Poppy insisted. "Nothing a bandage won't fix after we're not being shot at anymore." As another gunshot pinged against the boat, she squatted near the heater and pulled out her phone.

"I don't think we need to call the police," Thomas said. "If we can get out of range of that gun, we'll circle around to the main dock. There were be police there."

"I'm not making a call," Poppy said as she continued to fuss with her phone. She didn't offer any other comment, and Thomas was too busy driving the boat to press her.

He was grateful that the coroner wasn't a better marksman. He'd hit Poppy in the shoulder, but the bullets that struck the boat hadn't hit anything vital.

Once the shots stopped ringing out, Thomas checked on Poppy again. She'd stopped messing with the phone and simply held it loosely in her hand. "I'm surprised your phone works after being in the water."

"Waterproof case," she said, her tone dull.

"Are you sure you're all right?"

She nodded, though she was far too pale. "I'll be fine. Get us to the police."

The trip around the island would have been impossible in the midst of the storm, but it took mere minutes in clear weather. If their circumstances weren't so awful, Thomas would have enjoyed the sight of snow-covered stones along the shore. He normally loved the way snow softened the rough terrain of the island, but he was too cold and deeply worried about Poppy.

As he neared the main dock, he was surprised to see several officers there, including Detective Mortenson. Had he finished questioning everyone? Though it felt as if they'd been gone from the house for days, he knew it really had not been long. Had questioning been so cursory that it was done already?

He understood better when the detective raised a bullhorn and commanded Thomas to bring the boat into the dock, or be fired upon. "Why does everyone want to shoot us all of a sudden?" he asked, then cast an alarmed glance down when Poppy didn't answer.

She slumped over, her head hanging.

"We're almost there," he told her, wishing he dared stop and check on her.

They pulled up to the dock and Thomas knelt beside Poppy. "I'm all right," she mumbled, but he ignored her and lifted her into his arms.

When he stepped out on deck, every officer had a gun trained on him. "Dr. Vine is the killer," Thomas called to them. "He shot Poppy." He carried her across the deck.

"Put me down," she insisted, so he did. He could hardly jump onto the dock while holding her. He wouldn't risk it.

"Dr. Vine called me," Mortenson said as he strode over to the boat. "He told me he'd shot at the boat when you two tried to escape, so nice try."

"I'm telling you, Dr. Vine hired Cass Andrews and Betty Bing to kill my grandmother and her friends," Thomas said. "You need to arrest him."

"I'll decide what I need to do. Now keep your hands where I can see them and get off that boat."

Thomas hopped off, then helped Poppy down. She hissed sharply in pain at the jostling of her arm, but that was the sole sign of her pain beyond her pale face. She still clutched her cell phone, which struck Thomas as the oddest thing of all.

The detective pulled handcuffs out of his pocket. "Both of you, put your hands behind your back."

"She's been shot," Thomas protested. "And we aren't the killers. You need to arrest Vine."

Poppy held out her phone with a shaking hand. "Thomas is right, Detective Mortensen. Listen to this." She pushed a button on the phone and a recording began to play.

Mortensen took a step closer when he heard Dr. Vine's voice admitting that he'd murdered Matthew Bellamy. The recording continued, but Mortenson was already in motion, ordering officers to find and secure the coroner.

"He may be in the cove on the other side of the island," Thomas said, looping an arm around Poppy again to help her stay on her feet. "My mother's rental boat is tied up there. He might use it to try to escape. He has to know accusing us won't hold you for long."

The detective bobbed his head and ordered officers into one of the two police boats. He directed them to circle the island, retracing the way Thomas had come, and watch for the coroner. Before Mortenson joined them in the boat, he spoke to Thomas. "Thank you."

Thomas didn't respond, all of his attention on Poppy, who required more and more of his help to keep her feet. "She needs a doctor," he said.

"One is on the way," said a police officer close to them. "And there's a first aid kit in the other boat."

Poppy beamed into Thomas's face. "I told you I was fine." With that, she passed out.

18

"*May* I freshen your coffee? It's decaf," Arthur said as he leaned over the chair where Poppy rested in front of a fire.

"Thank you." She held up her coffee cup, surprised that even the movement of her good arm made her wound ache. She was grateful that she hadn't had to stay more than one night in the hospital but mildly disgruntled at missing Dr. Vine's arrest. The police had caught him trying to escape in Bethany's rental boat, exactly as Thomas had warned.

"Did the detective visit you in the hospital?" Mariette asked, waving away Arthur and the coffeepot. Arthur bowed slightly, then left the room.

"He did," Poppy said between sips of the excellent coffee. "But his tone was a lot nicer than during our earlier chats."

Thomas muttered something under his breath that Poppy didn't hear, but apparently Bethany did. "That's not fair," Bethany chided her son. "He's actually a good police detective. You have to admit, you both acted kind of guilty."

"I believe sneaking out to search the island was your idea," Thomas grumbled.

"Don't argue with your mother," Mariette said.

"Thank you, Mom," Bethany said. She and her mother exchanged a warm smile.

"Did Thomas tell you everything we found out from Dr. Vine?" Poppy asked.

The cheer vanished from Mariette's face. "He did. That horrible man killed poor Matthew. I'm going to miss my old friend terribly. All Matthew ever really wanted was a chance to do the right thing."

"He caused the right thing to be done," Thomas said. "That must count for something."

Mariette nodded. "I'm going to dedicate the memoir to Matthew. I was planning to dedicate it to Joseph, but that feels wrong in light of everything I'll be including in it."

"Especially considering Dad would have hated the fact that you're writing it at all," Bethany added.

"It's time for the truth to come out," Mariette said. "Matthew wanted it, even knowing he would face repercussions. And I want it too."

"It'll make trouble," Thomas said.

"And we'll weather it," Mariette said. "After the last few days, I think we could weather nearly anything." She patted Poppy's good arm. "Naturally, we'll wait until you're better. I know you're not in any condition to type."

"I'm fine," Poppy said. "And I can use talk-to-text to do the rough draft. By the time that's done, I should be completely healed to work on revisions."

"That's the spirit," Mariette said, beaming at her.

"There is something I've been wondering about," Poppy said. "How did Cass Andrews know about the secret room? I considered Mrs. Bing, but I don't know how she would have known about it."

"I showed Cass," Bethany said glumly. "We were kids, and I begged for a real birthday party with lots of kids. The only kids I knew were from town. Cass was my best friend's younger brother, so she brought him along. And I couldn't help but show off my secret room."

"I'm surprised he remembered that closet after all these years," Mariette said.

"Of course he remembered," Bethany said. "It was cool."

Mariette harrumphed, but even Poppy could tell neither of them was actually offended. It was part of who they were—two iron-willed women with strong opinions who didn't let that keep them from loving each other.

"I'm sorry I missed Cecil's departure," Poppy said.

"Surely you aren't," Bethany said. "He was about as cheery as ever. I think I heard three lawsuit threats on his way down to the dock."

"There will undoubtedly be a great many lawsuits," Mariette said. "Cecil's will be a drop in the ocean compared to the suits against our fortune when the horrible details come out about what Joseph and Cecil hired Dr. Vine to do. I never knew it was that bad." She shook her head. "I should have known."

"You can't fix what *should* have happened," Bethany said. "All you can do now is tell the truth and make amends where you can."

Her mother's expression danced between apology and mischief. "You do know that there won't be much inheritance left after all of this, don't you?"

"I don't want money made that way anyway," Bethany said. "I will be fine. And I think Thomas will be more than fine."

"Why?" Thomas asked. Then Bethany pointedly glanced from him to Poppy and back. Thomas's cheeks darkened, much to Poppy's amusement.

"I don't want to be rude," Mariette said, "but I'm a little tired. I had to give up my usual afternoon naps to be strong for my guests. I believe I'll simply be myself now."

"I'll walk up with you," Bethany said.

And Poppy watched mother and daughter walk out of the room, their heads tilted toward one another as they walked.

"They seem to have made up," Poppy said.

"Mom has taken a room closer to Mariette," Thomas said. "I think they have some catching up to do."

Poppy was glad for them. "I hate to admit it, but I might benefit from some sleep myself."

Thomas was beside her chair in an instant, almost startling her. He held out a hand. "Let me help you up."

"It's a bad shoulder," Poppy said. "My feet work perfectly fine." But she took his hand anyway, not wanting to come across as churlish.

He gently helped her up. "I still can't believe I nearly got you killed."

Poppy cocked her head to one side, peering up at his handsome face. "You didn't. I may have had some blood loss, but I remember clearly that it was Dr. Vine who shot me, not you." Then she grinned. "Though you did pull me off a cliff."

"That's not funny."

She laughed. "Everything is funny with enough distance."

"There isn't enough distance in the world to erase the sight of you stumbling into the boat's cabin with a bloody sleeve."

Poppy hesitated, not knowing any way to make it easier for him. She settled for changing the subject. "I assume you'll be leaving now."

"Why would you assume that?" he asked.

"Well, your mother is here to care for Mariette," Poppy said. "I thought you'd want to get back to the college."

"I'm on sabbatical," Thomas said. "And I'm in no hurry to cut that short. Besides, I have a new reason to want to be here on the island."

Poppy peered into his eyes, hopeful, but not sure his reason was what she wanted it to be. "And what's that?"

"You," he said.

And he took her face in his hands and kissed her. And Poppy discovered something else Thomas Nordwich did well. Very well.

Up to this point, we've been doing all the writing. Now it's *your* turn!

Tell us what you think about this book, the characters, the plot, or anything else you'd like to share with us about this series. We can't wait to hear from *you*!

Log on to give us your feedback at:

https://www.surveymonkey.com/r/InPeril

Annie's FICTION